FAIREST

A SAPPHIC FAIRY TALE

CARA MALONE

LISBON PRESS

ACKNOWLEDGMENTS

Thank you to my editor, Claire Jarrett, for never failing to challenge me and make me a better storyteller.

Thank you to Mayhem Cover Designs for the phenomenal book cover.

And thank you, always, to my readers, many of whom have also become friends. I appreciate each and every one of you!

LITTLE SNOW WHITE
BY JACOB AND WILHELM GRIMM

Once upon a time in midwinter, when the snowflakes were falling like feathers from heaven, a queen sat sewing at her window, which had a frame of black ebony wood. As she sewed she looked up at the snow and pricked her finger with her needle. Three drops of blood fell into the snow. The red on the white looked so beautiful that she thought to herself, "If only I had a child as white as snow, as red as blood, and as black as the wood in this frame."

Soon afterward she had a little daughter who was as white as snow, as red as blood, and as black as ebony wood, and therefore they called her Little Snow-White. And as soon as the child was born, the queen died.

A year later the king took himself another wife. She was a beautiful woman, but she was proud and arrogant, and she could not stand it if anyone might surpass her in beauty. She had a magic mirror. Every morning she stood before it, looked at herself, and said:

Mirror, mirror, on the wall,
Who in this land is fairest of all?

To this the mirror answered:

You, my queen, are fairest of all.

Then she was satisfied, for she knew that the mirror spoke the truth.

Snow-White grew up and became ever more beautiful. When she was seven years old she was as beautiful as the light of day, even more beautiful than the queen herself.

One day when the queen asked her mirror:

Mirror, mirror, on the wall,
Who in this land is fairest of all?

It answered:

You, my queen, are fair; it is true.

But Snow-White is a thousand times fairer than you.

The queen took fright and turned yellow and green

with envy. From that hour on whenever she looked at Snow-White her heart turned over inside her body, so great was her hatred for the girl. The envy and pride grew ever greater, like a weed in her heart, until she had no peace day and night.

Then she summoned a huntsman and said to him, "Take Snow-White out into the woods. I never want to see her again. Kill her, and as proof that she is dead bring her lungs and her liver back to me."

The huntsman obeyed and took Snow-White into the woods. He took out his hunting knife and was about to stab it into her innocent heart when she began to cry, saying, "Oh, dear huntsman, let me live. I will run into the wild woods and never come back."

Because she was so beautiful the huntsman took pity on her, and he said, "Run away, you poor child."

He thought, "The wild animals will soon devour you anyway," but still it was as if a stone had fallen from his heart, for he would not have to kill her.

Just then a young boar came running by. He killed it, cut out its lungs and liver, and took them back to the queen as proof of Snow-White's death. The cook had to boil them with salt, and the wicked woman ate them, supposing that she had eaten Snow-White's lungs and liver.

The poor child was now all alone in the great forest, and she was so afraid that she just looked at all the leaves on the trees and did not know what to do. Then she began to run. She ran over sharp stones and through thorns, and wild animals jumped at her, but they did her no harm. She ran as far as her feet could carry her, and just as evening was about to fall she saw a little house and went inside in order to rest.

Inside the house, everything was small but so neat and clean that no one could say otherwise. There was a little table with a white tablecloth and seven little plates, and each plate had a spoon, and there were seven knives and forks and seven mugs as well. Against the wall there were seven little beds, all standing in a row and covered with snow-white sheets.

Because she was so hungry and thirsty Snow-White ate a few vegetables and a little bread from each little plate, and from each mug, she drank a drop of wine. Afterward, because she was so tired, she lay down on a bed, but none of them felt right -- one was too long, the other too short -- until finally, the seventh one was just right. She remained lying in it, entrusted herself to God, and fell asleep.

After dark, the masters of the house returned home. They were the seven dwarfs who picked and dug for ore in the mountains. They lit their seven candles, and as soon as it was light in their house they saw that someone had been there, for not everything was in the same order as they had left it.

The first one said, "Who has been sitting in my chair?"

The second one, "Who has been eating from my plate?"

The third one, "Who has been eating my bread?"

The fourth one, "Who has been eating my vegetables?"

The fifth one, "Who has been sticking with my fork?"

The sixth one, "Who has been cutting with my knife?"

The seventh one, "Who has been drinking from my mug?"

Then the first one saw a that there was a little imprint in his bed, and said, "Who stepped on my bed?"

The others came running up and shouted, "Someone has been lying in mine as well."

But the seventh one, looking at his bed, found Snow-White lying there asleep. The seven dwarfs all came running up, and they cried out with amazement. They fetched their seven candles and shone the light on Snow-White. "Oh good heaven! Oh good heaven!" they cried. "This child is so beautiful!"

They were so happy, that they did not wake her up, but let her continue to sleep there in the bed. The seventh dwarf had to sleep with his companions, one hour with each one, and then the night was done.

The next morning Snow-White woke, and when she saw the seven dwarfs she was frightened. But they were friendly and asked, "What is your name?"

"My name is Snow-White," she answered.

"How did you find your way to our house?" the dwarfs asked further.

Then she told them that her stepmother had tried to kill her, that the huntsman had spared her life, and that she had run the entire day, finally coming to their house.

The dwarfs said, "If you will keep house for us, and cook, make beds, wash, sew, and knit, and keep everything clean and orderly, then you can stay with us, and you shall have everything that you want."

"Yes," said Snow-White, "with all my heart."

So she kept house for them. Every morning they went into the mountains looking for ore and gold, and in the evening when they came back home their meal had to be ready. During the day the girl was alone.

The good dwarfs warned her, saying, "Be careful about your stepmother. She will soon know that you are here. Do not let anyone in."

Now the queen, believing that she had eaten Snow-White's lungs and liver, could only think that she was again the first and the most beautiful woman of all. She stepped before her mirror and said:

Mirror, mirror, on the wall,
Who in this land is fairest of all?

It answered:

You, my queen, are fair; it is true.
But Snow-White, beyond the mountains
With the seven dwarfs,

Is still a thousand times fairer than you.

This startled the queen, for she knew that the mirror did not lie, and she realized that the huntsman had deceived her and that Snow-White was still alive. Then she thought, and thought again, how she could kill Snow-White, for as long as she was not the most beautiful woman in the entire land her envy would give her no rest.

At last, she thought of something. Coloring her face, she disguised herself as an old peddler woman, so that no one would recognize her. In this disguise, she went to the house of the seven dwarfs. Knocking on the door she called out, "Beautiful wares for sale, for sale!"

Snow-White peered out the window and said, "Good day, dear woman, what do you have for sale?"

"Good wares, beautiful wares," she answered. "Bodice laces in all colors." And she took out one that was braided from colorful silk. "Would you like this one?"

"I can let that honest woman in," thought Snow-White, then unbolted the door and bought the pretty bodice lace.

"Child," said the old woman, "how you look! Come, let me lace you up properly."

The unsuspecting Snow-White stood before her and let her do up the new lace, but the old woman pulled so quickly and so hard that Snow-White could not breathe.

"You used to be the most beautiful one," said the old woman, and hurried away.

Not long afterward, in the evening time, the seven dwarfs came home. How terrified they were when they saw their dear Snow-White lying on the ground, not moving at all, as though she were dead. They lifted her up, and, seeing that she was too tightly laced, they cut the lace in two. Then she began to breathe a little, and little by little she came back to life.

When the dwarfs heard what had happened they said, "The old peddler woman was no one else but the godless queen. Take care and let no one in when we are not with you."

When the wicked woman returned home she went to her mirror and asked:

Mirror, mirror, on the wall,
  Who in this land is fairest of all?

The mirror answered once again:

You, my queen, are fair; it is true.
  But Snow-White, beyond the mountains
  With the seven dwarfs,
  Is still a thousand times fairer than you.

When she heard that, all her blood ran to her heart because she knew that Snow-White had come back to life.

"This time," she said, "I shall think of something that will destroy you."

Then with the art of witchcraft, which she understood, she made a poisoned comb. Then she disguised herself, taking the form of a different old woman. Thus she went across the seven mountains to the seven dwarfs, knocked on the door, and called out, "Good wares for sale, for sale!"

Snow-White looked out and said, "Go on your way. I am not allowed to let anyone in."

"You surely may take a look," said the old woman, pulling out the poisoned comb and holding it up. The child liked it so much that she let herself be deceived, and she opened the door.

After they had agreed on the purchase, the old woman said, "Now let me comb your hair properly."

She had barely stuck the comb into Snow-White's hair when the poison took effect, and the girl fell down unconscious.

"You specimen of beauty," said the wicked woman, "now you are finished." And she walked away.

Fortunately, it was almost evening, and the seven dwarfs came home. When they saw Snow-White lying on the ground as if she were dead, they immediately suspected her stepmother. They examined her and found the poisoned comb. They had scarcely pulled it out when Snow-White came to herself again and told them what had happened. Once again they warned her to be on guard and not to open the door for anyone.

Back at home the queen stepped before her mirror and said:

Mirror, mirror, on the wall,
Who in this land is fairest of all?

The mirror answered:

You, my queen, are fair; it is true.
But Snow-White, beyond the mountains
With the seven dwarfs,
Is still a thousand times fairer than you.

When the queen heard the mirror saying this, she shook and trembled with anger, "Snow-White shall die," she shouted, "if it costs me my life!"

Then she went into her most secret room -- no one else was allowed inside -- and she made a poisoned, poisoned apple. From the outside, it was beautiful, white with red cheeks, and anyone who saw it would want it. But anyone who might eat a little piece of it would die. Then, coloring her face, she disguised herself as a peasant woman, and thus went across the seven mountains to the seven dwarfs. She knocked on the door.

Snow-White stuck her head out the window and said, "I am not allowed to let anyone in. The dwarfs have forbidden me to do so."

"That is all right with me," answered the peasant

woman. "I'll easily get rid of my apples. Here, I'll give you one of them."

"No," said Snow-White, "I cannot accept anything."

"Are you afraid of poison?" asked the old woman. "Look, I'll cut the apple in two. You eat the red half, and I shall eat the white half."

Now the apple had been so artfully made that only the red half was poisoned. Snow-White longed for the beautiful apple, and when she saw that the peasant woman was eating part of it she could no longer resist, and she stuck her hand out and took the poisoned half. She barely had a bite in her mouth when she fell to the ground dead.

The queen looked at her with a gruesome stare, laughed loudly, and said, "White as snow, red as blood, black as ebony wood! This time the dwarfs cannot awaken you."

Back at home, she asked her mirror:

Mirror, mirror, on the wall,
Who in this land is fairest of all?

It finally answered:

You, my queen, are fairest of all.

Then her envious heart was at rest, as well as an envious heart can be at rest.

When the dwarfs came home that evening they

found Snow-White lying on the ground. She was not breathing at all. She was dead. They lifted her up and looked for something poisonous. They undid her laces. They combed her hair. They washed her with water and wine. But nothing helped. The dear child was dead, and she remained dead. They laid her on a bier, and all seven sat next to her and mourned for her and cried for three days. They were going to bury her, but she still looked as fresh as a living person, and still had her beautiful red cheeks.

They said, "We cannot bury her in the black earth," and they had a transparent glass coffin made, so she could be seen from all sides. They laid her inside, and with golden letters wrote on it her name, and that she was a princess. Then they put the coffin outside on a mountain, and one of them always stayed with it and watched over her. The animals too came and mourned for Snow-white, first an owl, then a raven, and finally a dove.

Snow-White lay there in the coffin a long, long time, and she did not decay but looked like she was asleep, for she was still as white as snow and as red as blood, and as black-haired as ebony wood.

Now it came to pass that a prince entered these woods and happened onto the dwarfs' house, where he sought shelter for the night. He saw the coffin on the mountain with beautiful Snow-White in it, and he read what was written on it with golden letters.

Then he said to the dwarfs, "Let me have the coffin. I will give you anything you want for it."

But the dwarfs answered, "We will not sell it for all the gold in the world."

Then he said, "Then give it to me, for I cannot live without being able to see Snow-White. I will honor her and respect her as my most cherished one."

As he thus spoke, the good dwarfs felt pity for him and gave him the coffin. The prince had his servants carry it away on their shoulders. But then it happened that one of them stumbled on some brush, and this dislodged from Snow-White's throat the piece of poisoned apple that she had bitten off. Not long afterward she opened her eyes, lifted the lid from her coffin, sat up, and was alive again.

"Good heavens, where am I?" she cried out.

The prince said joyfully, "You are with me." He told her what had happened and then said, "I love you more than anything else in the world. Come with me to my father's castle. You shall become my wife." Snow-White loved him, and she went with him. Their wedding was planned with great splendor and majesty.

Snow-White's godless stepmother was also invited to the feast. After putting on her beautiful clothes she stepped before her mirror and said:

Mirror, mirror, on the wall,
Who in this land is fairest of all?

The mirror answered:

You, my queen, are fair; it is true.
But the young queen is a thousand times fairer
than you.

The wicked woman uttered a curse, and she became so frightened, so frightened, that she did not know what to do. At first, she did not want to go to the wedding, but she found no peace. She had to go and see the young queen. When she arrived she recognized Snow-White, and terrorized, she could only stand there without moving.

Then they put a pair of iron shoes into burning coals. They were brought forth with tongs and placed before her. She was forced to step into the red-hot shoes and dance until she fell down dead.

1

LUMA

I can't believe he took my phone.

That was the detail Luma White was focused on as she sat in the passenger seat of her Audi, hands bound in front of her and a blindfold slipping down around her nose. Her phone – how much of an eighteen-year-old girl could she be? *That* was what she was most concerned about, but on the other hand, it was easier to fixate on the phone than on everything else.

She'd been in the car for about three hours now. The blindfold – made of some ridiculously silky fabric, definitely not kidnapping-grade – had begun sliding down her nose about an hour into the trip and she was grateful for that. Riding in a car with her eyes shut always made her feel sick, and when her captor noticed that she could see again, she convinced him not to cover her eyes again.

"I'm already lost," she said. "Isn't that why you blindfolded me? So I wouldn't know where we're going? Mission accomplished."

The man driving Luma's car was her stepmother's bodyguard, Antonio. Slave would have been a more appropriate word for how that woman treated him, but he'd always been nice to Luma.

Well, until today.

At least she was going to get through this without being sick. *Silver linings and all that.*

They were driving on a narrow, somewhat primitive road with tall, evergreen trees on either side. It was dark thanks to the forest's dense coverage even though they started driving around noon. Antonio had appeared in the doorway of Luma's room and told her he needed help running an errand for her father – that was a little unusual, but nothing to raise her suspicions. By the time he was opening the passenger door of Luma's car for her, telling her they were going to pick up some files at her father's office, Luma started asking questions. *How did you get my car key?* was the first one, but she never got an answer to that.

Once she was in the car, Antonio locked the doors and told her to put the blindfold on. Luma objected, and that's when things got scary. He'd forced the blindfold over her eyes and she'd spent the first whole hour of the trip frantic.

The errand to her father's office was a lie and

16

Luma should have seen it coming – Antonio worked for her stepmother, and her father was out of the country. Luma hadn't even questioned it when Antonio said it was for her father.

If Luma was thinking clearly, she should have been memorizing the turns of the car, listening for sounds outside that could help her, and keeping better track of the time. But she'd known Antonio ever since she was a kid – since her stepmother, Tabitha, did her Vogue modeling spread and picked up a stalker in the process. She hired Antonio to keep her safe, and Luma always felt safe around him, too.

Now, she was just scrambling to try and figure out what had changed.

Was he kidnapping her?

"Where are you taking me?" she'd asked before she realized the futility of demanding that sort of information from someone who'd blindfolded her. When she got her wits about her a little more, she asked, "Why do I have to be blindfolded? Did Tabitha ask you to do this? What are you going to do to me?"

Antonio didn't respond to any of her questions. He was dead silent from the driver's seat, and when Luma's blindfold began slipping down her nose, she could see that his eyes never strayed from the road ahead. *Please just look at me,* she thought. *What are you doing?*

Her last-ditch attempt to snap him out of whatever

had overcome him was a threat that sounded weak even to Luma's own ears. "Wait until my father hears about this."

"Shut up," Antonio said. "Please, just keep your mouth *shut*."

It wasn't a favorable response, but at least he'd said something. His words sounded almost as pleading as Luma's own questions, like he was frantically trying to find a way to justify all of this. Tabitha had to be behind it. Of course – Tabitha had always hated her.

So Luma shut up, and she waited.

She tried to be patient and wait for Antonio to come to his senses. He'd do the right thing – she just had to give him time to come to his senses. He'd abducted his boss's stepdaughter while her husband was out of town on business. Antonio was probably just trying to figure out how to take Luma home without letting her father know what he'd done.

Or rather, what Tabitha had ordered him to do.

It had to be the stupid modeling contract, Luma thought while Antonio drove them deeper and deeper into the woods. *Damn it. I don't even* want *to be a model.*

Tabitha had blown up at her yesterday. She'd gone downtown in the morning to get her lips plumped and the aesthetician had used a new type of filler. Tabitha's lips had blown up like balloons and she came home looking like she had a pair of plump red hotdogs beneath her nose. They looked painful and she was irritable, and then she'd seen the contract that Luma had left on the desk in her father's study.

Luma wanted him to review it when he came home from his business trip. She'd never imagined herself as a model, never wanted that kind of attention, but people kept saying she was beautiful and it was a natural fit for her. She'd gone to the modeling agency mostly to humor the agent who kept trying to recruit her, and because she was eighteen now and she still didn't know what she wanted to be when she grew up.

Why not a model? she thought when they offered her the contract. So she brought it home and promised the agency an answer just as soon as she had a chance to discuss it with her father.

Then Tabitha saw the contract and lost it. Luma had never seen her so angry, actual spittle flying from her over-puffed lips as she slammed the contract down in front of Luma.

"You don't even *want* to be a model," she said, narrowing her eyes at Luma. "You don't want your trust fund, either. You don't appreciate anything you've got, and it's all just been *handed* to you. Ungrateful girl!"

Tabitha hadn't spoken to Luma since yesterday, but the longer Antonio drove, the more certain she was that this was all Tabitha's doing. *Am I ungrateful?* she was wondering for the hundredth time when the car hit a pothole and she could no longer ignore the fullness of her bladder.

"Antonio?" she asked softly.

"Don't talk," he said.

"Antonio," she insisted, trying not to anger him. "I really have to pee. I can't hold it much longer."

She looked at him, and for once, he looked back at her. She was begging him, wordlessly. *Please. On top of everything else, please don't put me through the humiliation of wetting myself.* He hadn't listened to anything else she said so far, but the desperation in her eyes was what finally cracked him.

He sniffed, then looked at the clock on the dashboard – probably trying to figure out how far they'd come from the house. Far enough – Luma's father loved to be in the middle of the action and he'd built his mansion in the center of the city. Luma had never even been this far into the wilderness and it might as well have been a whole other country.

"Fine," Antonio said. "Hold on a minute."

"Thank you," Luma said. "Thank you, Tony."

He scowled at her. Was that too much, calling him by his nickname? He never minded it before, but he'd never abducted her before, either. Antonio found a dirt road that branched off the two-lane highway and turned onto it. *Road* was pretty generous, actually – it was barely more than a couple of grooves worn into the dirt. He drove the car just far enough so that it wouldn't be seen from the road, then turned off the engine.

The passenger door unlocked automatically and Luma reached for the handle, but Antonio locked it again with the push of a button on the driver's side door. "I'm coming around to get you."

"Okay," Luma squeaked. When he opened the door from the outside, he extended his hand to help Luma out – probably more through instinct than anything else. She took his hand, shaking her head so the blindfold fell all the way down to her neck, and she said hopefully, "You know, Tabitha gets in her moods all the time. I bet by the time we drive home, she'll have forgotten what she was mad about."

"Do you have to pee or don't you?" Antonio asked.

"Yeah, I do," Luma said. "But-"

She wanted to know what he was thinking. There was a wild, cornered look in his eyes that she really didn't like, and things suddenly felt a whole lot more dire now that the two of them were standing alone in the great silence of the forest.

"Go, then," he said. "There's a bush right over there."

"Okay," Luma said meekly.

Her bladder really was aching – she'd just finished a pretty big smoothie when Antonio came into her room and she'd been squirming in her seat for quite a while. Trying *not* to think about how badly she had to go was the only thing that had been distracting her from the awfulness of the situation, but she couldn't ignore it anymore.

She went behind the bush, the heels of her shoes sinking into the soft earth and pine needles poking her bare legs as she lifted her skirt. Just as she was beginning to feel a bit better – about one thing, at least – she heard the Audi's engine roar to life.

Oh, God, he's leaving me out here!

Luma rushed to rearrange her skirt and darted out from behind the bush just in time to see Antonio floor the gas pedal. The tires spun in place for a moment, kicking up dirt and moss from the forest floor, and then the car gained traction and Antonio drove it straight into a tree.

"What the hell?" Luma shouted as the hood crumpled slightly and the engine died. A small tendril of steam was rising from the car and Luma ran around to the driver's side. "Antonio, are you okay?"

She got there just in time for him to open the door – he had to put his shoulder into it since the collision had bent the frame of the car. He got out, unscathed, and Luma looked at him wide-eyed and speechless.

Antonio put his hands on her shoulders, their eyes locking as he said, "Your stepmother ordered me to bring you out here and kill you. I've been going over it in my head for the last three hours, trying to imagine a world in which I could do that, and I just can't."

Tabitha wants me dead?

A jolt of fear ripped through her, followed by a

twinge of relief. Antonio said he couldn't do it - so where did that leave them? Standing next to the smoking remains of Luma's car, that was where. No matter what else happened, they weren't going to be driving out of there.

"Listen carefully," Antonio said. "You met with the modeling agency yesterday. They sent you on a go-see and that's where you were going today – you were driving alone, a deer jumped in front of your car and you crashed. You must have been disoriented – maybe you hit your head. You wandered into the woods and no one heard from you again."

"But Antonio-"

"Tabitha has her eyes on your trust fund," he continued. "You know that, right?"

"I know she hates getting an allowance from my father," Luma said, swallowing hard. "But this is about the modeling contract, isn't it?" He shook his head and Luma had never seen him so serious. "She really wants me dead?"

"I've been her right hand for ten years," Antonio said. "I know her better than anybody and I know when she's serious about something. Luma, you have to disappear or she will kill you."

"What about my dad?" she asked. "Let's call him, or-"

Or the police, she thought.

"I can't do that," Antonio said, glancing at the car. "You don't know what she's capable of."

"I think I have some idea," Luma said, crossing her arms over her chest. She had no phone, no money, and no idea where she was. If she screamed at the top of her lungs right now, no one but the birds and other forest animals would hear her – and Antonio, who'd already made up his mind.

"No," he said, shaking his head. "You really don't. Trust me, Luma, for your own safety – and mine – you have to let Tabitha think you're dead. If you come home, she'll kill you and then she'll kill me for not doing the job myself."

Luma's mouth dropped open as she attempted to process all of this, trying to formulate a response that never materialized.

"Just disappear, Luma," he said. A tear ran down his cheek and he added, "I'm sorry."

He turned and started walking back toward the road, and Luma called after him, "Antonio." When he turned around, she asked, "Are you planning to walk home?"

"I'll figure something out," he said. "So will you."

Shit. Antonio turned around and headed back up the dirt path to the highway, and Luma just stood in the forest for a minute, trying to wrap her mind around what just happened.

She tilted her head back, feeling a headache coming on. The forest was actually kind of beautiful, shafts of sunlight breaking through the evergreens and highlighting the pine needle-carpeted forest floor.

A bird chirped, unseen, in a tree somewhere close and Luma thought it sounded like a cuckoo. Her high school biology teacher had been obsessed with birdsong and Luma had a lot of them memorized even though she'd rarely heard them in real life. Cuckoos weren't city birds.

"What the hell am I supposed to do now?" she asked the forest, and because the trees didn't talk and birds rarely sang their songs in English, she received no answer.

She went over to the car and tried the key in the ignition, but the engine was shot and it wouldn't turn over. She went through the glove compartment and the trunk, looking for anything that could help her, but she'd never been more than a phone call away from AAA. The glove compartment held nothing helpful and Luma was all but useless without her phone, anyway.

She was stranded and she had no choice but to start walking. Her heels kept sinking into the loamy forest floor as she picked her way back up the overgrown dirt path and she was actually relieved when she got to a paved road. Her kitten heels weren't made for hiking, but at least she could get her footing on the road.

At least I'm alive.

That was not a thought she expected to have that day. She kept walking, trying not to focus on all of the questions stretching out on the road in front of her.

Where am I going? What will I do when I get there? Do I go to the cops? Will Tabitha retaliate against Antonio – or even my dad – if I do?

They were all unanswerable, insurmountable problems.

And then Luma started to hear pine needles crunching in the forest beside the road. She turned her head and for a fleeting moment, she wondered if Antonio had a change of heart and was coming back for her.

Or coming back to finish the job. Tabitha always did have an otherworldly ability to know when her demands were not being met. She was a woman of means and beauty – or at least she used to be – and it was pretty rare that anyone dared to disobey her. Did Antonio call her after he crashed Luma's car? Did he cave already and admit that he hadn't done what Tabitha asked of her?

Then all of those worries dissipated and Luma's heart arrested in her chest.

A fat black bear was lumbering toward her out of the forest, no more than thirty feet away. It turned its head sideways at her, wondering how it had gotten so lucky that its next meal had delivered itself to the woods. Its mouth opened, a hint of long, sharp teeth poking out from under its lips, and then Luma was running.

The bear emerged onto the road, looking like it didn't mind chasing down its dinner. Luma ran as fast as her feet would carry her, and when one of her heels fell off, she barely gave it a thought. She limped a few steps and then kicked off the other shoe, hardly losing speed.

She made it about fifteen yards away and then a second bear emerged from the woods, standing in front of her. If a bear could speak, this one would have said, *Gotcha.*

Are you freaking kidding me? Luma thought.

When the bear in front of her growled, she ducked off the open road and through a tangle of what turned out to be pricker bushes. They cut into her bare arms and legs, but Luma fought her way through them. Her stepmother put a hit on her, her father was away on business, and Antonio had just smashed her car. She was *not* about to be eaten by bears on top of everything else.

Luma didn't turn around to find out if the bears were giving chase. She didn't acknowledge the pain of each pine needle stabbing into the tender soles of her feet, or the scratches and pinpricks of blood covering her arms and legs. She just ran until her lungs burned and her thighs ached, until she had to stop or else she'd fall down in exhaustion.

When she finally did stop, leaning against a tree and panting to catch her breath, Luma looked back. There were no bears, and there was no visible path back to the road. She couldn't see the road at all anymore, and she couldn't even say with any certainty which direction she'd come from.

"I'm lost," she said to the forest, tears springing to her eyes. "I am lost in the woods."

She might not have spent much time in the forest before, but Luma knew from her schooling that it went on for hundreds of miles. People got lost in the forest every year, some of them died, and Luma was no Girl Scout.

She sank to the ground, her skirt riding up her thighs as more pine needles jabbed into her skin. She put her head back against the tree and her long black hair snagged against the rough bark. She looked up. The only thing she had going for her was the fact that it was spring, the days were getting longer, and she still had a good five hours of daylight left – not that she had any idea what to do with it.

Then, above the tall trees, she noticed a thin tendril of smoke in the distance.

Luma watched it for a minute or two, expecting it to disappear, but it persisted – it was a sign of life and her best shot at survival. She got up, brushed the pine needles off her skin, where they were stuck to her by a thin sheen of sweat, and started walking.

Limping was more like it, and she winced with every step. Her shoes were lying on the side of the road, or perhaps had become a bear's new chew toys. She had no choice but to pin all her hopes on that tendril of smoke.

If she was lucky, it was the smoke from someone friendly's fireplace.

What she found, at least an hour and many, many painful pine needles later, was a cottage in a clearing. It was all by itself in the woods, no sign of civilization nearby, and the smoke trail Luma had followed was coming from a large brick structure outside the cottage. It was about six feet square – a fireplace of some sort closed on all sides with a large steel plate on the front that looked like a door, plus a chimney on top.

"Hello?" Luma called. Her voice echoed softly against the trees but no one answered.

She left the fireplace and walked around to the cottage door. Someone had swept the dirt around the perimeter of the building, a welcome reprieve from the pine needles that had rendered Luma's feet numb.

She knocked on the door, waited and listened for a minute, then called, "Hello? Is anyone home?"

No one answered. Luma tried to peek in the windows, but they were covered with a film of dirt and she couldn't see inside. If it wasn't for the smoking fireplace, she would have thought the cottage was abandoned.

She knocked again, then tried the doorknob.

It turned easily and the door swung inward. Luma called again, "Hello? I'm sorry to intrude, but I could really use some help."

There was still no answer, and she glanced back toward the forest, then down at her own scraped and dirty limbs. It was either stay outside and risk another encounter with those bears or go inside and hope the cottage had a telephone. At the very least, she could get cleaned up and dig the pine needles out of her feet.

Luma inched her way inside.

2

CHARLIE

The sun was just beginning to go down when Charlie Jacobs came walking along the footpath that led to the cottage. She had an ax slung over her shoulder and her face was dirty with the effort of the day.

She was following her six older brothers, bringing up the rear of the single-file line that they were forced into thanks to the narrowness of the path. Charlie's oldest brother, Scotty, carried a chainsaw, and the two brothers closest to her age – Thomas and Joey – were carrying a four-foot crosscut saw between them. Everyone else had an ax over his shoulder and a lunch bag in the other hand. Ever since Charlie joined the family lumberjack business last month, they'd been working on clearing a section of the forest about a mile away from the cottage.

"Dibs on the shower," Scotty said as they entered the clearing around the cottage.

He was thirty-five but he still broke into a childish run toward the house, pushing his glasses up on the bridge of his nose as he raced Charlie's second-eldest brother, Adam. They both made a mad sprint toward the cottage, Adam laughing as they wedged shoulder-to-shoulder in the doorway.

Charlie just shook her head, watching the two of them fight to keep each other from squeezing through the door. In her nineteen years, she'd never met anyone more competitive than the two of them. *I bet I can chop down my tree first. I bet I can finish my sandwich before you. Race you to the truck.*

The rest of them headed over to a woodshed where they stored all their tools each night and put away all the axes and saws that they'd used that day. Charlie handed her ax to her brother, Braden, then said, "I'm going to go check on my kiln."

In the Jacobs family, chivalry wasn't so much dead as it had never existed – at least when it came to Charlie. From the day she was born, the youngest and the only girl in a big family, she had been just one of the guys. She knew from experience not to expect any special treatment, and that meant she'd be waiting in line for the shower just like everyone else.

The water would probably be icy cold by the time she had her turn, and there was a good chance that Adam or Thomas would accidentally use Charlie's towel and she'd have to dry off with a hand towel instead.

It wasn't that they were mean or careless – but they weren't going out of their way to make her feel welcome in the family business, either. Everybody seemed to think they knew better than Charlie when it came to what she should be doing, and everyone – from her brothers to her parents – told her she was a fool to drop out of college last year.

"But you're so smart," Charlie's mom had said when she came home after her spring final exams and announced that she would return in the fall over her own dead body.

Her mom thought she was wasting her potential. She'd put her index finger up to Charlie's forehead then, tucking a strand of tawny hair out of her eyes. Charlie stepped back, letting her locks fall back down over her forehead.

She didn't even really like to keep her hair long – it was forever in her eyes, a liability for someone who made her living swinging an ax. But there was a large, deep pink scar that covered half of her forehead and came down over her left eyelid, and keeping her hair long was the best way Charlie had found to keep people from staring too blatantly.

Her scar was from laser treatments she'd undergone as a kid – a hemangioma birthmark had bloomed over her left eyebrow as a baby and grew rapidly to cover nearly a quarter of her face. Her parents had taken her to a specialist in the city when she was two years old because the birthmark was threatening the vision in her right eye, and the treatment had worked, but it left her with an ugly scar.

Her mother had frowned when Charlie flinched away and said, "You're beautiful. You know that, right?"

"This has nothing to do with that," Charlie lied. "I want to go into the family business. If it's good enough for all your other kids, then why not me?"

Because you're our little girl. Because you've always been great in school and because you have a scholarship —you could write your ticket to whatever career you want. Those were answers Charlie had heard over the last month, ever since she moved out of her parents' house in Grimm Falls and come to the forest to work with her brothers.

Out here, no one cared if her face was messed up. No one cared if she was pretty, or what she'd scored on her SATs. And despite all the other subjects that her brothers loved to tease her about, the scar had always been off-limits.

Out here, she got to just be Charlie.

"Yeah, go check on your kiln," her middle brother, Maxwell, said. "You might wanna cuddle up to that pottery because there's not gonna be any hot water left in the shower."

Charlie rolled her eyes and reminded him, "I have

six older brothers. I've never taken a hot shower in my *life*."

She walked around to the side of the cottage, where her brick kiln was still releasing a few tendrils of smoke into the afternoon sky. Despite his protests, Charlie's dad helped her cart her pottery wheel from Grimm Falls out to the cottage.

It really was ideal, having a kiln built in the woods, so close to the source material of her craft. The clay out here was way better than the stuff Charlie bought in the craft store in town, and that was another good reason to quit college and move to the forest – now that she had a fully functioning kiln, she'd begun to turn her favorite hobby into a little side business. Her pottery already had quite a following among the locals in Grimm Falls.

Charlie had promised Scotty that she'd be a hard worker, a fast learner, and an asset to the family business, but in the evenings, she was free to follow her true passion. She put on a heat-resistant glove now and pulled open the small door on the side of the kiln, peeking inside.

The embers burning in the bottom were still red hot, and the dozen hand-turned clay vases curing on the shelf looked just about ready to come out. Charlie regularly jogged back to the cottage on her lunch breaks to stoke the fire, opening or closing the chimney to regulate the heat, and this round of vases would be cool and ready to come out by morning. She left the kiln door open and opened the chimney all the way to let the fire burn out, then headed into the cottage.

Ordinarily, Adam or Scotty would get in the shower first – depending on who won that day's race – Braden would be dozing on one of the couches, and Maxwell, Joey and Thomas would be sitting down to play whatever shoot-em-up video game they were obsessed with at the time.

Today, all six of them were standing around the open door to Charlie's bedroom.

I swear I closed that this morning, she thought as she walked through the living room, annoyed that one of them must have been rooting through her stuff.

She lifted her feet on instinct to avoid the trip hazards of shoes and other detritus that always littered the living room floor, then noticed that was different, too. She looked around and saw a couple pairs of shoes lined up in front of the hearth, and the coffee table had been neatly arranged, too. *Weird.*

"What's going on?" she asked, and Maxwell shushed her. Charlie arched an eyebrow at him, then elbowed her way into the doorway.

"You have a houseguest," Adam said.

"What?" Charlie started to ask, and then she caught sight of her bed—and the girl fast asleep in it. She had her hands tucked under her cheek and her chest was rising and falling peacefully. Her skin was like porcelain and her hair was a beautiful, silky black.

"Do you know her?" Braden asked.

Charlie gave him an *Are you crazy?* look. "No, of course not."

Her hand went automatically to her bangs, rearranging her tawny hair carefully over her forehead. The girl's eyes were shut, not a hint of tension in her porcelain face despite the fact that seven people were staring at her. Charlie thought she detected a slight smile on her ruby-red lips.

Was she having a good dream?

"She's hot," Adam said, and Charlie drove her elbow into his ribs. He wheezed as he asked, "What was that for?"

"For being rude," Charlie said, although Adam wasn't wrong – even with her eyes closed, this was easily the most beautiful girl Charlie had ever seen. In Grimm Falls, or on movie screens - there were no qualifiers necessary.

She was overwhelmingly pretty and she was sleeping in Charlie's bed.

"What's she doing here?" Charlie whispered.

"She's waiting for you, obviously," Joey smirked.

They might have drawn the line at teasing Charlie over her birthmark, but girls were most certainly *not* off-limits. They were one thing Charlie and her brothers could agree on, and the Jacobs siblings seemed to believe that the best way to get back on the horse after heartbreak was a good ribbing about the dismal state of one's love life.

"Waiting for Charlie?" Adam whispered. "No way. That's a straight girl if I ever saw one."

"*Have* you ever seen one?" Scotty asked him.

"Shut up," Adam retorted.

"Both of you shut up," Charlie said, trying to keep them quiet as the girl's brows furrowed slightly. She stirred but didn't wake, and Charlie noticed that her arms – as porcelain white as the rest of her complexion – were crisscrossed with angry pink scratches. What happened to her? And what were they going to say – or do – if this strange girl woke up to find all seven of them staring at her? "Come on, let's go out to the living room."

"Shouldn't we wake her up?" Joey asked. "Find out what she's doing here?"

"Let her sleep," Charlie said, pulling her door shut to give the girl some peace.

"She is technically trespassing," Maxwell pointed out.

"I think she's in trouble," Charlie said as they all sat down on the three large couches arranged in a U-shape in the living room. "Did you see the scratches on her arms?"

"Yeah," Scotty said, nudging his glasses back up his nose again. "We should let her sleep. She'll come out when she's ready, and then we can find out what she's doing here."

"I'll start dinner," Braden said, getting up and going to the kitchen in the corner of the large, open space. He pulled a large stock pot from beneath the sink and started filling it with water, then said, "Hope everyone's hungry for spaghetti."

"Again?" Joey asked with a groan.

"I think I'm allergic," Thomas said.

"You're allergic to everything," Braden said, rolling his eyes.

"Okay, then, I'm just plain sick of it," Thomas amended. "What is that, the second time this week?"

"If you want to cook something different, be my guest," Braden said. "Otherwise, we're having spaghetti."

Scotty got up to take his shower – it turned out he'd won the race but got distracted by the girl in Charlie's bed. Maxwell asked whether someone should be keeping guard over the girl, just in case she decided to steal something, and Adam let out a guffaw that echoed through the room.

As they went through their customary evening routines, all of them kept an eye on Charlie's bedroom door, waiting for the girl to emerge. She never did, and Charlie wondered if she'd woken up, heard so many voices talking on the other side of the door and panicked. The girl might have gone out the window hours ago for all they knew.

Charlie was the last to shower, as predicted, and she did it fast for two reasons. One, the water was just as icy as it always was. And two, the longer they all waited for the girl to come out of her room, the more curious Charlie got. She didn't want to miss the excitement if she came out while Charlie was in the shower.

Charlie washed the dirt of the forest off her skin and used the small mirror over the sink to slick her bangs back down over her eyes. Over the last month, she'd gotten out of the habit of combing her hair forward because the only people who saw her on a day-to-day basis were her brothers, but tonight, she wanted to make sure her birthmark was covered. She didn't want that to be the first thing the girl saw when she met Charlie.

She's probably straight like Adam said, she chastised herself before she left the bathroom and found her brothers gathered around the long dinner table, already helping themselves to spaghetti.

"Shit," she said.

"What?" Scotty asked from the table.

Charlie glanced at her bedroom door. She had her hand clutched around her chest, holding her towel up. "My clothes are in there."

She always got dressed in her bedroom, and it hadn't even occurred to her until she'd stepped out of the shower that it wasn't an option tonight.

"So go in and get them," he said, completely unperturbed.

"Would you want to wake up to find a stranger in a towel rooting around in the dresser?" Charlie asked.

Adam just shrugged and said, "Better you than one of us."

Yeah, he had a point there. She took a deep breath and tiptoed over to her bedroom door. She opened it slowly, part of her hoping to find her bed empty after all.

But the girl was still there, still sleeping peacefully.

Damn, she sleeps like a rock, Charlie thought as she pulled the door closed behind her to mute the sounds coming from the dinner table. She crept over to her dresser, uncomfortably close to the bed. There was a window over the headboard and the light was beginning to turn orange and pink as the sun went down. It cast a pretty glow over the girl's fair skin and Charlie's breath caught in her throat as the girl's tongue snaked momentarily out to moisten her plump lips.

Charlie lingered to admire her beauty for a moment. The girl was harmless while she was asleep, incapable of noticing Charlie's birthmark, let alone curling her lip in disgust the way Charlie was all too used to watching people react.

But she would probably die right then and there if the girl's eyes opened to see her standing over her bed in nothing but a towel. So she returned her attention to the task at hand, wincing as the dresser drawer squeaked. She grabbed the first shirt and pair of jeans she came across, plus a pair of underwear and a bra, and then high-tailed it back out of the room.

She closed the door, her clothes clutched to her chest like Indiana Jones having just escaped the boulder, and Adam cackled at her from the table.

"Is she still asleep?" he said.

"Yeah," Charlie said, rolling her eyes. "I'm going to get dressed. Save me some spaghetti."

"No promises," Braden said as Charlie headed back into the bathroom.

3
―――

LUMA

The next time Luma opened her eyes, the moon was shining through the window above her. It was full and bright, and once her eyes adjusted to it, she twisted in the bedsheets to look into the room.

It was small, just enough room for a twin bed, dresser, and a small rug on the floor. The sheets she was wrapped up in were soft cotton and they smelled faintly of pine – of course, everything out here smelled like the forest.

The cottage had been empty when she first arrived. It had a large common area, with three large couches circled around the fireplace and a long dining table nearby. The place was a mess, with shoes scattered across the floor and dishes piled in the sink, and when Luma went into the bathroom to clean up, she found a row of seven toothbrushes in a custom holder.

There were plenty of signs of life, but no people.

No phone, either, that Luma could see.

She found a washcloth in a drawer beneath the sink and used it to scrub the dirt and blood from her arms and legs. She was still covered in angry red scratches from the pricker bushes, but she felt a little better.

Her ears had been tuned in the whole time she was in the bathroom, her body on high alert and listening for any sign that the occupants of the cottage had returned – or worse, the bears. But no one came so Luma hung the washcloth over the edge of the sink to dry and went back into the common area.

This cottage was her best chance of getting help, so she decided to wait until someone came home. She occupied herself by tidying up the living room – it was the least she could do since she was in someone else's home. She lined up the shoes and washed the dishes in the sink. By the time the living room was put to rights, there were still no signs of the cottage's occupants and Luma started poking around the rest of the space.

Maybe there was a phone in one of the bedrooms and she'd just missed it. She hadn't noticed a phone line attached to the house, but she might get lucky and find a cell phone. She found four bedrooms in the cottage – a master with twin beds, a couple of rooms with bunk beds, and the little room with the twin-sized bed she was laying in now. Seven beds to match the seven toothbrushes, and not a single cell phone or anything else that might help her. Even if she'd found a phone, she wasn't sure she could call the police.

By the time she got to the last bedroom, Luma was feeling exhausted in body and mind. Everything that had happened to her was beginning to sink into her bones and she collapsed in the small bed, burying her face in the pillow and willing herself not to cry.

You'll figure this out, she told herself. *It can't be as bad as it seems. Your stepmother tried to kill you, you lost your shoes running from bears, and you have no idea where you are. But maybe the people who own this cottage will help you.*

Then the tears came, and she must have fallen asleep mid-sob.

Now, the cottage was dark and quiet, and Luma started to wonder if it was abandoned after all. She sat up in bed and noticed light moving in the gap beneath the door. She trained her ears and heard the crackling of a fire in the hearth, but nothing else.

She got up quietly, adjusting her skirt and smoothing the blouse that had wrinkled and twisted around her torso as she slept. She winced as she padded her way across the hardwood floor – the pine needles biting into her bare feet had been painful with every step through the forest, and now her soles were tender and swollen from those hundreds of pinpricks.

Luma opened the bedroom door slowly, her heart

climbing into her throat as she wondered what – or who – she would find. *Whoever you are, please don't kick me out in the middle of the night.*

She saw the fire first, flickering in a large stone hearth. It was spring and the hardwood floor was a little chilly, which actually felt pretty good on her sore feet. The fire was the only source of light in the living room and it appeared to be unattended. The doors to the other three bedrooms were all shut, and Luma padded quietly around the end of one of the couches.

Stretched out on it, with a knit blanket across her chest and her bare feet poking out the bottom, was a girl about Luma's age. *The rightful owner of the twin bed?*

The fireplace cast Luma's shadow across the girl's face when she got near and the change in light startled her awake. When she saw Luma, she jolted upright and the blanket fell around her waist.

"Hi," Luma said, taking an apologetic step back. "I'm sorry I woke you."

"Look out," the girl said, her eyes going wide.

"What?" Luma asked just as her heel caught on a very large hiking boot left haphazardly on the floor and she lost her balance. She started to fall backward, arms pinwheeling as the heat of the fire licked her back.

Then the girl's hand closed around Luma's wrist and she pulled her back to her feet. She overcompensated, pulling Luma to her chest and wrapping her arm protectively around Luma's waist. She was an inch or two taller than Luma, and significantly more muscular. The cut of her biceps was obvious even through her long-sleeved t-shirt and she had a strong grip.

Her hair was wild from sleeping on the couch, a pretty light brown that offset startling aquamarine eyes. Above her left brow, the girl's skin took on a darker hue, and the moment she noticed the direction of Luma's gaze, she let go of her and smoothed her bangs down over her forehead.

"I'm Charlie," she said. "You were sleeping in my bed."

"Oh," Luma mumbled. "I'm sorry."

"It's fine," Charlie said quickly. "I just- that's why I was on the couch. Sorry about the boots, I know you cleaned up, but my brothers are kinda feral."

Luma smiled. She was the one intruding in Charlie's home, rearranging her living room and putting her out of her bed, and yet Charlie was the one getting flustered. It was cute, but Luma needed to put her at ease.

She smiled and said, "I'm Luma. I really appreciate you letting me sleep in your bed because I had a hell of a day yesterday."

"Are you okay?" Charlie asked.

Those eyes caught the light of the fire like the facets of a gemstone as they studied Luma, flitting down to the scratches covering her arms. She didn't really know how to answer that question. "I think so. It's a long story."

"Sit down," Charlie said, motioning to the couch. "Do you want something to eat or drink?"

On cue, Luma's stomach rumbled audibly, as if it had been saving all its complaints for a moment when she could actually do something about it. She let out a small laugh and said, "Yeah, I guess so."

"I can make you a sandwich," Charlie offered. "Do you like turkey?"

"I like anything right now," Luma said.

Charlie's hand went to her bangs again, and then she went over to the kitchen in the corner. Luma followed her instead of sitting on the couch and while Charlie pulled ingredients out of the refrigerator, Luma sat down at a bar stool on the other side of a large island.

While Charlie assembled two turkey sandwiches, one for each of them, Luma said, "You mentioned your brothers. How many do you have?"

"Six," Charlie said. That accounted for the other six beds Luma had found, and the seven toothbrushes, but...

"What about your parents?" she asked. "Do they live here, too?"

"No, they live in Grimm Falls, about five miles from here," Charlie explained. "You're currently in the headquarters of Jacobs Lumberjacks – my oldest brother, Scotty, runs the business and the rest of us work for him. I just started last month."

"The only girl in the family?" Luma asked, intrigued as Charlie slid one of the plates across the island to her and then got her a glass of water to go with it.

"Yep," Charlie said. "Lucky me. What about you? You don't look like you're from around here."

Luma was right in the middle of a big, unladylike bite of her sandwich and she covered her mouth when Charlie caught her stuffing her cheeks. She hadn't eaten since that smoothie around noon, and that wasn't much of a meal. Charlie took a big bite of her sandwich, too, and waited patiently.

Luma swallowed, then said, "Thanks for the sandwich. Mm, it's really good." She let her posture relax a little bit, slouching on the bar stool as she filled her belly, and Charlie's cheeks colored slightly when she moaned. Then she said, "You're right – I'm not from around here. I live in Rockledge."

Or I did... Luma tried not to think about that as she downed her water in one long swallow, then Charlie went to the sink to refill her glass.

"You're far from home," she said. When she came back to the island, she walked around it to set down Luma's water. She glanced momentarily at her bare thighs, then her eyes met Luma's as she asked, "How did you get all scratched up?"

"Would you believe me if I said I was chased by a couple of bears?"

"I believe you, but that's really unlucky," Charlie said. "The bear population around here is small – you must have met two of only about fifty bears in the entire forest."

"That's really just the tip of the iceberg when it comes to my luck lately," Luma said. If she told this girl everything about what happened to her yesterday, would she believe it? Would she insist they call the cops before Luma figured out the best way to handle the situation?

Well, there's no phone here, anyway...

She took another bite of her sandwich and Charlie sat down on the bar stool next to her. She looked bashful, but those gemstone eyes were dancing with light reflected from the fireplace. She seemed to have forgotten about her own midnight snack, half-eaten on the other side of the island, and instead, she was studying Luma. She was taking in her scratched arms and legs, the outfit that screamed *wasn't planning to go for a hike today*, and Luma's bare feet.

She waited patiently until Luma finished her sandwich, then she asked, "Do you need help? I could drive you into town – there's a police station in Grimm Falls."

"No," Luma said abruptly. "I can't go to the police yet."

"What happened?" Charlie asked.

Luma shook her head. "It's going to sound crazy."

Then Charlie backed off, sliding off her bar stool and saying, "You don't have to tell me. It's really none of my business. For now, can you just tell me whether you're in danger?"

"I don't think so," Luma said, letting out a sigh of relief.

There was no way she could find the words for a conversation with a stranger about how her stepmother got jealous of her modeling contract and tried to have her killed for her trust fund. It didn't even sound real to Luma – there was no way Charlie would understand it.

"I think if I can just lay low for a little while, it'll blow over and I can go home," she said, more to herself than to Charlie. Tabitha had gotten angry at her hundreds of times when Luma was a kid, with varying degrees of consequence. None had ever been this bad, but she'd always gotten over it eventually.

I just need time.

"I can't speak for my brothers," Charlie said. "We'll have to run it by Scotty in the morning, but as long as he's okay with you staying, I don't mind giving up my bedroom."

"Oh, that's not what I meant-" Luma started to say, embarrassed, but Charlie waved off her objections.

"There are six big lumberjacks sleeping in those bedrooms, plus me. We all have axes and we can be an intimidating bunch if we need to be," she said. "If someone's trying to hurt you, we'll keep you safe."

Tears welled in Luma's eyes, coming out involuntarily for the second time that day. She slid off her bar stool, wincing as her feet hit the floor, then put her arms around Charlie's neck. Charlie flinched, unprepared for the hug, and Luma let her go. The last thing she wanted to do was make her guardian angel uncomfortable.

"Thank you," she said. "You have no idea what it means to have someone be nice to me right now. I was so lost."

Charlie looked away from her. She was obviously not used to big displays of emotion, and maybe that had something to do with being raised with six brothers. She composed herself and then joked, "Well, as long as you leave us a good Yelp review."

Luma laughed, then took a few steps toward the kitchen sink, intending to wash the dishes they'd just dirtied. She was walking tentatively, trying to be careful of her tender feet, and Charlie noticed.

"Are you hurt?"

"Just my pride," Luma tried to joke, but Charlie followed her around the island.

"You were out there barefoot," she said. "Let me see."

"My feet?" Luma asked, surprised.

"Yes," Charlie demanded. So Luma put her hand on Charlie's shoulder to steady herself and lifted the sole of one foot for her to see. There was no ladylike way to do it and she had to use her hand to keep her skirt from sliding up her thigh and giving Charlie more of a view than she'd bargained for. She focused her attention on Luma's foot, though, and clucked her tongue. "That looks pretty raw. Go sit down on the couch and I'll get you something for your feet."

"I was going to wash the dishes," Luma objected. "It's the least I can do-"

"Sit," Charlie repeated. "I'll wash them."

Luma did as she was told, mildly amused at being ordered around the cottage by a lady lumberjack with gemstone eyes. Charlie disappeared into her bedroom, then into the bathroom, and came back a minute later with a bottle of lotion and a pair of soft slippers.

"Looks like they're a size or two larger than you wear, but it beats walking around on the hard floor," she said as she handed the slippers and the lotion to Luma.

"Thank you," she said. "Really."

Charlie stayed with Luma for the rest of the night.

Luma tried to convince her to reclaim her bed and get a few good hours of sleep, but Charlie didn't want to leave her alone without knowing exactly what brought her to the cottage and who might be after her... and Luma was secretly relieved to have Charlie watching over her.

The fire died down and the two of them dozed off. Luma dreamed about being reunited with her mother – it was a recurring one that she often had when she and Tabitha clashed. Her mother always appeared at the height of Tabitha's cruelty, banishing her and taking her rightful place as the matriarch of the family. It was comforting, but it could only ever be a dream because Luma's mother had died in childbirth.

The next time Luma woke, her head was on Charlie's shoulder and a strange man was standing in front of the couch, staring at her.

Luma sat up and Charlie woke beside her. The man – a few years older than Charlie but undoubtedly one of her brothers by the distinct color of his eyes – said, "Getting cozy with our houseguest, huh, Charlie?"

She looked embarrassed and distanced herself from Luma. She made a big show of standing up to stretch, then took a few steps away from the couch like they'd done something they shouldn't have.

"This is Luma," she said. "Luma, my brother, Maxwell."

"Nice to meet you," Luma said, extending her hand to him. But his eyes were narrowed and he was regarding her with suspicion. He shook her hand, making it clear that he was doing so reluctantly.

"What are you doing here?" he asked as he let go.

"Relax," Charlie said, patting Maxwell's shoulder. "She just needs a place to stay for a little while. She's not here to steal your video games, or whatever it is you're thinking."

Luma gave Charlie an appreciative smile – she wasn't looking forward to telling her story seven separate times until every Jacobs sibling knew what happened to her. She wasn't even sure *she* understood it, but sooner or later she was going to owe her hosts some sort of explanation.

The rest of Charlie's brothers woke up and came out of their bedrooms in ones and twos. Luma was grateful not to have to meet all of them at once – seven names was a lot to memorize when she was still trying to orient herself in this new, post-murder-attempt reality. Charlie did her best to introduce each of them as they trickled out of their rooms and began their day.

There was Scotty, the eldest, who looked like he was in his mid-30s and wore a pair of thick-framed glasses. He seemed imminently responsible and gregarious.

Next was Adam, one year younger than Scotty and far less serious. Luma was pretty sure he was flirting with her when he shook her hand and made smoldering eye contact. He had the same aquamarine eyes – they all did – but Charlie's were the only ones that made Luma feel warm and fuzzy when they fell on her.

Braden was one of the middle brothers, emerging from his bedroom with a yawn and looking like he could use another four or five hours of extra sleep. He'd said hello and shuffled into the kitchen to start a pot of coffee. Luma watched with amusement as he pulled a second entire coffee maker out of a lower cabinet and used that one, too. One pot of coffee would hardly be sufficient for seven people, or eight now that Luma was there.

Maxwell continued to give Luma probing, distrustful looks as he moved about the kitchen, laying nearly an entire loaf of bread on a pan to make toast.

Thomas was in his twenties, with a large beard befitting a lumberjack. He sneezed right after Charlie introduced him to Luma, then apologized and grumbled about seasonal allergies as he wandered off to the bathroom.

And last but not least, there was Joey. One year older than Charlie at twenty, he had a baby face and a clear craving for attention. He talked loudly so that his voice would carry through the cottage, and nearly everything out of his mouth was a joke tailored to whoever was listening at the time.

By the time breakfast was on the table and all the Jacobs siblings were dressed for a day of work, Luma was feeling overwhelmed. There were a lot of names to remember and a lot of big personalities bouncing around the cottage and making it feel smaller than it was. Luckily, Charlie retrieved her from the couch, bringing her over to the table.

"Have my seat," she said. "I'll grab one of the chairs we use when our folks come to dinner."

She went to a closet near the kitchen and brought a folding chair over to the table, squeezing in between Luma and Adam. Everyone passed serving dishes of eggs, bacon and toast around, and Luma stared in wide-eyed wonder at the amount of food these guys heaped on their plates.

She was nibbling a piece of crispy bacon when Scotty asked, "So, Luma, Charlie says you're from Rockledge. That's a few hours away. How'd you get way out here?"

"You weren't hiking in *that*, were you?" Maxwell asked, nodding to her skirt. She was still wearing the slippers Charlie had given her last night, and her feet really did feel a lot better now that they were moisturized and padded.

"I wasn't hiking," she said. *Oh boy, here goes...* "I got into a fight with my stepmother."

That seemed like the easiest way to describe what happened.

"Did you run away?" Scotty asked, pushing his glasses up his nose. He looked like the concerned older brother type – not that Luma would know as an only child.

"No," she said. "I'm eighteen."

The last thing she needed was a mistaken call to Child Services or the police. She glanced at Charlie, who had been so understanding last night, telling her she didn't need to explain anything she wasn't ready to tell her. But these people had all been so nice to her, feeding her and showing no signs of wanting to kick her out. She had to tell them the truth.

"My stepmother and I have never gotten along," she said. "She's a jealous woman and it's only gotten worse the older I get – well, the older *she* gets, really. Yesterday, I got something that she always wanted but couldn't have, and she lost it. She ordered her bodyguard to bring me out here and kill me."

There were a couple of gasps around the table, Thomas put his hand to his mouth and muttered in shock, and Charlie's eyes went wide.

Adam put his hand over Luma's on the table and she had no more doubt about the fact that he was interested in her. She discretely took her hand back under the guise of taking a sip from her coffee mug, a unique earthenware piece that looked handmade.

"Your stepmom put a hit on you?" Joey asked. "Damn."

"What did she want?" Braden asked.

Aside from my trust fund? Luma thought. "She used to be a model. She did okay with it but the biggest job she ever had was the cover of Vogue in the late 70s. She got a stalker out of it, hence the bodyguard, but everyone else lost interest and moved on. What Tabitha wanted more than anything was a contract with a high-profile modeling agency that could have really catapulted her career." Luma paused, looking at Charlie. *Goodbye, relatability.* "The agency my stepmom always wanted to work for offered me a contract and it sent her into a jealous rage. I knew she was angry, but I didn't realize she could be dangerous, too."

Luma looked around the table. Every single one of the Jacobs siblings was smiling empathetically at her, even the grumpy Maxwell. She knew why – it was the same reason her stepmother resented her, the same reason a modeling contract that she didn't even *want* had fallen into her lap.

Luma was pretty.

Beautiful, a lot of people said.

She knew she could trade on her looks, use them to stay here for as long as she wanted because when she looked around the table, it was obvious in the blue-green eyes of each and every Jacobs sibling – they wanted her. Luma was nice to look at, and that alone could get her pretty far in life. Tabitha had been getting by on her looks for decades and that was probably why she was so insufferable now – her looks were fading and she had nothing to fall back on but an ugly personality.

But Luma didn't want to stay here on those terms. She didn't want her career to be handed to her on a silver platter. She wanted someone – anyone – to see her for more than just a pretty face. And even though she desperately needed some charity right now, she didn't want to take it from the Jacobs siblings on those terms.

She had to have *something* else to offer.

Her lower lip quivered and she was on the verge of tears again. *No. I will not cry anymore.* Then she felt Charlie's arm around her shoulders. It was comforting like she had been last night, and it was just enough to chase away the tears.

4

_____

CHARLIE

Charlie was barely even aware of the choice to put her arm around Luma's shoulders.

She'd sworn off all intimacy that had to do with women when she quit college and came to live in the forest, but sitting next to Luma, watching the tears begin to collect on her lashes, Charlie knew it was what she needed.

"It's okay," she said softly. "We'll keep you safe."

From the other end of the table, Scotty was being pragmatic as always. "One of us can take the day off and drive you into town so you can talk to the police. We don't have a phone – no landline would stretch all the way out here and our cell phones don't get reception. But it's a short drive to Grimm Falls."

"I can't go to the police," Luma said, fear springing to her eyes. She'd had the same strong reaction last night when Charlie suggested it, and she wasn't budging on the topic. "My stepmother's bodyguard told me if I came back, if she found out I wasn't dead, she'd finish the job herself and then she'd kill him, too."

"But if the police are involved-" Braden started to say, but Luma was in a near-panicked state at the idea.

"No," she said. "Tabitha snapped, and now I don't know what she'll do." She took a deep breath, closing her eyes for a moment and Charlie could tell she was wrestling with herself. "I have a sizable trust fund and apparently my stepmother has her eyes on it. If she's going after the money, I don't know what she'll do to get it. She could hurt her bodyguard or my father. I have to disappear like Antonio told me to."

"Antonio?" Adam asked on Luma's other side.

"Tabitha's bodyguard," Luma clarified. She looked around the table, then locked eyes with Scotty, pleading with him. "Please let me stay here, just until I can figure out what to do next. I promise I won't get in the way, and I could even cook and clean for you."

She glanced at the living room. It didn't take long for seven messy people to undo all the tidying she'd done yesterday and the sink was already full of dishes from the morning meal.

Charlie tore her eyes away from Luma and snuck a glance around the table. Her brothers all seemed to be drawn to her the same way Charlie was – like mosquitos to the irresistible pull of a bug zapper. Beautiful and dangerous.

Even after everything she'd been through – which

sounded like the plot to a horror film – and then having to deal with the entire Jacobs clan at once, Luma was poised and graceful. Her silky black hair was smoothed neatly down and her round eyes were bright and optimistic against all odds.

Charlie admired that, and when Luma's gaze fell on her, she became very self-conscious of where her arm was. She removed it from Luma's shoulders, then shook her head so her bangs fell properly over her forehead. It was a habit that had turned into a nervous tick, something she barely even thought about anymore but which was suddenly at the forefront of her mind now that Luma was here.

"What if her bodyguard comes back to finish the job?" Maxwell asked.

"We'll protect her," Charlie answered automatically.

"Thank you," Luma said. "Anyway, he doesn't know where I am. He crashed my car on the side of the road to make it look like an accident, but I don't even know what road that was. I ran through the woods for a long time before I got to your cottage. I think I'm safe as long as I can stay here."

"You can stay as long as you need to," Scotty said, and Luma visibly relaxed in her chair.

"Thank you," Luma said. "I promise I won't be dead weight."

"Don't worry about that," Scotty said, nudging his glasses up again. "Just let us know what you need."

"Nothing," Luma said quickly. "Your hospitality is more than enough."

"Everybody dig in," Braden said, picking up the serving plate of bacon and sending it around the table again. "We have to clear that big white oak today and get the lumber order ready for the Wilsons' new construction job. There's still work to be done despite everything else going on."

Luma smiled apologetically at him. "I don't want to throw off your schedule. Pretend I'm not even here."

"You're no bother," Adam reassured her, reaching for a few more pieces of bacon.

"So, what exactly do you do out here in the forest?" Luma asked as everyone ate. "Charlie says you're lumberjacks."

"Yep," Scotty said proudly. "Third generation. Our grandpa built this cottage with his own hands, settled in the woods and made himself a business of supplying the lumber when Grimm Falls was being built."

"Our dad was a lumberjack, too," Charlie said. "But Mom told him she wasn't raising seven kids in the forest, so they moved into town and Dad kept up the business by driving out here every morning. He's retired now, but all of us have worked in the business in some way since we were kids."

"When Dad retired, he gave us all shares of the business, and he left Scotty in charge as the oldest," Braden explained. "One by one, we all graduated from high school and moved out here to work in the family trade. None of us has kids and only Joey and I have girlfriends in town, so it made sense to come back and run the business from the cottage again instead of commuting. This way we're right in the middle of the action."

Joey snorted and said, "As much action as there is in the forest."

"I got chased by bears yesterday," Luma said, surprisingly jovial about it. "I'd call that action."

"Wow, you *did* have a crazy day," Maxwell said, finally cutting Luma a little slack.

When the meal was over, everyone piled their plates beside the sink and Luma offered to wash them while the siblings were working. Charlie went over to the refrigerator and set up an assembly line of lunch meats, bread and condiments, and Luma offered to help.

"I'm going to stay here with you today," Charlie said as they made twelve turkey sandwiches – two for each of her brothers – and packed them inside six lunch bags along with soda cans and apples from the fridge. "Unless you'd rather have one of my brothers stay behind?"

"No," Luma said, and Charlie stifled a smile. "It sounds like you have a lot of work to do, though. What about the white oak tree?"

"My brothers will get along without me," Charlie said. "I don't want to leave you alone here."

"Afraid I'll steal Maxwell's video game collection?"

Luma asked with a smile. She was joking, but Charlie could see the vulnerability in her eyes.

"No," Charlie said, completely serious. "I'm afraid your stepmother or her bodyguard will come back for you. I know it's not really my business, but you slept in my bed last night. That makes me feel responsible for you."

Luma's porcelain cheeks turned the prettiest color of light coral, then she looked away as the brothers started grabbing their lunch bags.

"What's the plan?" Adam asked.

"I'm going to stay with Luma," Charlie said. "You'll have to make do without me for the day."

"I'm sure we'll manage," Maxwell said. "We'll probably get more work done without you holding us back."

"Oh man, look who just lost his soda privileges," Charlie said, grabbing for his lunch bag.

Maxwell was faster, snatching it off the table and muttering, "Jerk."

"Are you two going to be okay here by yourselves?" Scotty asked.

Charlie looked to Luma for reassurance, although it probably should have been the other way around, then said, "We'll be fine."

"Yeah," Luma agreed.

Scotty said, mostly for Luma's benefit, "We'll be back around sundown. If you need any help, one of you is going to have to come get us."

"We'll be fine," Charlie reiterated, and then the guys all marched outside. Luma went to the door to watch them leave, stopping in the doorframe because she was still in Charlie's slippers. Her feet swam in them and she had to shuffle as she walked – it was cute, but only a small step up from being barefoot.

Charlie came up behind her, careful not to crowd her as they watched her brothers go to the woodshed and pull out the tools they'd need for the day. They grabbed axes, sledgehammers and chainsaws. All the wood splitting and planing tools they would need were already at the job site under a tarp.

The six Jacobs brothers headed into the woods, walking single-file along the narrow path they always took. Someone at the front of the line was whistling – it was either Scotty or Adam who always started it. Before they were out of earshot, most of the others had joined in.

Then Luma and Charlie were alone in the cottage. Luma turned in the doorway to face her, and Charlie was grateful for the gentle breeze that cooled her face as Luma said, "Thanks for staying with me."

5

TABITHA

"What took you so long?" Tabitha asked Antonio as soon as she'd pulled him into the privacy of her dressing room. They were the only two in the house at the moment, but she wasn't about to risk some servant showing up to pick up dry cleaning and overhearing this.

It was more than 24 hours after she'd sent Antonio on his mission and she'd been on the edge of her vanity seat ever since.

"I'm sorry," he said. "There were... complications."

"What?" Tabitha snapped. Then she held up her hand. "I don't want to know about them - just tell me, is she dead?"

"Y-yes," Antonio stuttered. His eyes shifted away from her.

"What did you do with the body?" She demanded. "Buried?"

She knew he wouldn't have the stomach for this kind of stuff – his value as a bodyguard was mostly in his pliability. He'd do anything Tabitha said without question.

"Err, no," he said.

"*What?* Why not?"

"Well, I made it look like an accident," he said, gaining his confidence.

Good, Tabitha thought. There was nothing she hated more than a sniveling coward, and if they were going to get away with this, she needed him on top of his game.

"I figured that'd be the easiest way to avoid questions," Antonio explained. "I drove her out to the forest and crashed her car into a tree, and then I-" There was that shiftiness again. Pathetic. "I took her into the forest and hit her over the head."

"You're sure she's dead?" Tabitha asked.

"Yes, ma'am," Antonio said.

"*Madam,*" Tabitha corrected him. "What do I look like, an eighty-year-old?"

She studied him for a moment and he was still having a hard time meeting her eyes. Probably feeling guilty. She'd have to work *that* out of him before the news of Luma's untimely, tragic death hit the media. Couldn't very well have a suspicious-looking bodyguard lurking around in the background while Tabitha was speaking to the press.

"Good," she said, pushing past him to the large

mirror at her vanity. She picked up a red lipstick and leaned into the mirror, carefully applying it over her swollen lips as she said, "Now we wait for the police to find her car, and then the body. Lucca will be home in two days and he already texted me a half-dozen times to ask where the little brat is – said she didn't answer her phone all day yesterday."

"I have it," Antonio said, pulling it out of his pocket and lighting up as if Tabitha was going to give him a treat for being such a good little doggie. *Should I drop down on my knees in my eight-hundred-dollar dress and thank him? Fat chance.*

He handed the phone to Tabitha and she tossed it on top of the vanity. She'd deal with that later. She looked at him through the mirror – waiting for a cookie, perhaps?

"Well?" she snapped. "You're dismissed."

"Yes, *Madam*," he said, then scurried out of the dressing room. She waited until he was gone, then turned her attention back to herself. The bad fillers were already beginning to look better – the swelling was going down and it didn't look so obvious anymore that the aesthetician had been pinching back a sneeze when she stabbed Tabitha in the wrong place.

"I'm still beautiful," she murmured to herself as she put the lipstick back in its place among dozens of others.

She nodded, affirming her own words, then pulled a tissue out of a nearby box to remove the shade from her lips. She'd thought *Cherries in the Snow* would be right, but now she was thinking *Better Off Red* would be best to disguise her bruised and swollen lips.

———————

Tabitha hoped that her husband would come home from his business trip before he started asking questions about the girl. With any luck, the police would find the car just as Lucca got home from Hong Kong, and the two of them could go through the grieving process together.

It would be so much easier if Tabitha could just mirror Lucca's emotions and pretend she gave a shit about the little wretch.

Of course, nothing could ever be easy and Lucca started worrying pretty much immediately. *And the Overprotective Father of the Year award goes to...*

"I've texted her a half-dozen times and called her twice. You *know* how teenagers are glued to their phones," he told Tabitha over the phone later that night. "I'm worried about her."

"Sweetheart, you need to let that girl grow up," Tabitha said, putting on the nicest, most concerned voice she could muster. "She's eighteen years old and she's going to want her independence."

If only the spoiled girl had come to that conclusion herself and gotten out of Tabitha's sight on her eighteenth birthday, maybe they wouldn't be in this situation. Figuring out how to get her hands on the sizable trust fund would be Tabitha's consolation.

"It's not like her not to text back for a whole day," Lucca insisted.

Tabitha rolled her eyes. The brat's phone was tucked into the drawer of her vanity, turned off and the battery removed so it couldn't be tracked. She wondered if she should just turn it on and text Lucca on his daughter's behalf. Honestly, who needed to speak to their grown daughter this often? Once a week was *more* than enough.

But she couldn't risk creating more questions than necessary about the timeline of Luma's death. If Tabitha used her phone and the police did all their forensic tricks once they found the body, they might start asking questions about what kind of dead girl sends text messages.

Tabitha managed to calm Lucca down and get him off the phone, but by the next morning, he was calling her back, talking about changing his flight plans.

"It isn't like Luma to drop off the map like this," he said. "She could have been in an accident. She could be lying in a hospital room somewhere, wondering why no one's coming for her. Are you *sure* you don't know where she went?"

"I'm sure she's not in a *hospital*," Tabitha said. *A morgue's more likely.* "Sweetheart, you know Luma and I have never really been close. She doesn't tell me things the way she opens up to you."

She'd almost slipped up right there and said *She never told me anything.* Past tense. Murderers used the past tense, but Tabitha's hands were clean.

"When you're not in town, it's not unusual for her to disappear for a few days," Tabitha fibbed. "You know what I just remembered? Gosh, I feel so stupid not thinking of it earlier. The last time I saw her, she mentioned a modeling agency contract. She wanted you to look it over when you got home."

"She wants to model?" Lucca asked skeptically.

Tabitha gritted her teeth. "I don't know. They talent scouted her, as far as I could tell."

That was probably the part that hurt the most. The pretty little idiot didn't even *care* about what was being handed to her – what Tabitha had spent her whole career fighting tooth and nail for.

Her stepdaughter was ungrateful and she didn't even *know* she was ungrateful. She didn't deserve any of it—the contract, the money, that face. Tabitha grimaced, then caught her reflection in her vanity mirror and forced her facial muscles to relax. That was how one got wrinkles.

"That's great," Lucca said, cautious optimism edging into his voice. He was so eager to latch onto the little branch of hope Tabitha was extending to him, he didn't even question why it had taken her two days to remember this. "So you think she's busy with modeling stuff?"

"Could be," she said, reaching for a jar of wrinkle cream.

This whole process was going to be tedious and she hadn't counted on that. First, they'd find the car. Then they'd have to search for Luma. Then when they found the remains, Tabitha and Lucca would have to go through all that grieving stuff. There would be funeral plans and Lucca would probably be sullen and moody for *months* after...

"Well, I'm going to have my assistant book me an earlier flight regardless," Lucca decided. "I have one more meeting scheduled for tomorrow, but it's not a critical one – I can make it a video call from the plane."

"If you think that's best," Tabitha said. "I'm sure by the time you get back, Luma will be home."

In a box, or an urn depending on how long it takes them to find the remains.

6

LUMA

Luma and Charlie spent their first day alone together in the cottage cautiously getting used to each other. Luma's nerves were frayed after what she'd been through and Charlie seemed skittish and unsure of herself. Luma busied herself with cleaning things up around the cottage as a way to repay the Jacobs siblings' kindness to her, and in the afternoon, she and Charlie raided the refrigerator to make dinner for when Charlie's brothers got home from their work.

The eight of them spent the night hanging around the living room and Luma played video games with Maxwell, Thomas and Joey to keep her mind off her circumstances. She slept in Charlie's bed again, feeling guilty for displacing her as she slipped into another dream about her mother.

On her second morning in the cottage, Charlie

offered to stay behind with Luma again. After her brothers had gone off to work, Luma brought Charlie a refill for her coffee mug and asked, "Are you sore from sleeping on the couch?"

Charlie rustled her bangs and said, "No, it was fine."

"Well, I won't put you out of your bed again tonight," Luma said. "Point me in the direction of the washing machine and I'll clean the sheets for you. I'll take the couch tonight."

"You're a guest," Charlie objected. "Guests don't sleep on the couch."

"Guests aren't usually strangers who show up unannounced and throw your life out of whack," Luma countered.

"You're not throwing my life out of whack," Charlie said. Then she smiled. "Okay, you are. But I don't mind."

No, you don't – because I'm pretty, Luma thought. She wasn't going to let Charlie and her brothers give her special treatment, though. She went into Charlie's bedroom and Charlie followed her, continuing to object as Luma pulled the sheets off the bed.

"Luma, please," she said. "Take the bed again tonight. You don't have to do this."

Luma balled the sheets in her arms and turned around. "If I don't focus on cleaning your sheets, I'm going to have to think about the fact that my step-mother tried to have me killed and my dad is probably worrying that he hasn't heard from me in two days. Please, let me wash your sheets."

"Okay," Charlie relented. She stepped aside from the doorway and said, "The washing machine is in the closet beside the bathroom."

Luma went into the hall and found the door Charlie was referring to. She stuffed the sheets into the washer, then said, "What about your brothers' sheets? They probably don't get cleaned too often, do they?"

Charlie snorted. "I've been here a month and I've never seen anyone wash their sheets."

"Well, that's an easy fix," Luma said. "I can help with that."

She and Charlie went from room to room, stripping the beds and making a huge pile of laundry in front of the washing machine. They stuffed as many sheets as they could into the first load, then Luma turned on the machine and looked at Charlie with her hands on her hips.

"Feel better?" Charlie asked.

"A little," Luma admitted. "We should wash the towels, too."

She padded into the bathroom and she wasn't wincing as often when she walked. That was a good sign, but she definitely needed a pair of proper shoes. And that skirt, which grazed her thighs as she walked, was pretty chilly in the evenings.

When Luma came back with seven bath towels and a couple of hand towels in her arms, she dropped them on top of the growing laundry pile and said, "I couldn't help noticing you have exactly seven of everything here."

"It's a relatively small cottage for seven people," Charlie said. "There's not much room for redundancy."

Luma sighed. "I can't keep putting you out like this."

"We'll make room for you as long as you need it," Charlie said. "And you're not putting me out. The couch is actually pretty comfortable."

"I can't just stay here forever," Luma said. Damn it, there were those stupid tears threatening again! Suddenly, she was crashing into Charlie, putting her arms around her because that was the only time she'd felt safe in the last forty-eight hours. She barely knew Charlie, but she felt protected in her midst, and she needed to let her vulnerability out now or else she'd implode with all the tension.

Charlie hesitated at first and Luma could feel her tensing, wondering whether to pull away. But then she put her arms around Luma and the ground felt a little more stable for the moment.

"My dad's going to be worried sick about me when he gets home from his business trip and I'm not there," she said. He was scheduled to return from Hong Kong the next day and Luma had never gone so long without at least texting him.

Then what? What was Tabitha going to tell him?

Had she even thought that far ahead, or did her collagen-riddled mind jump to the first violent act she could think of and fail to plan the whole thing out?

"And then there's Antonio," she said. "God knows what she'll do to him."

"Are you worried about him?" Charlie asked, surprised. "He brought you into the forest to kill you."

"Because Tabitha told him to," Luma said, pulling away from Charlie and drying her eyes. "He didn't do it, though. He's a good guy working for a horrible woman, and if she finds out he didn't actually kill me, she might take it out on him."

Or Tabitha could be relieved that he didn't follow through on her hot-headed plans. That was probably the best Luma had to hope for – maybe her step-mother would send Antonio back into the woods to retrieve her before her father found out what happened.

Maybe staying put *was* what she needed – at least for right now.

She put her hands over her face. "Oh, Charlie... I don't know what to do."

"We should go into town and buy you some shoes, at least," Charlie suggested. "Whether you stay here or not, you're going to need shoes. And some warmer clothes."

"No," Luma said quickly. "Antonio told me to disappear. I can't be seen and risk it getting back to my stepmother."

"I could go for you-" Charlie started to suggest, but Luma interrupted.

"Don't leave me alone," she said.

"Okay," Charlie said. "I'll stay with you."

"I'm sorry," Luma said. "I'm a mess and I'm ruining your whole week."

"You're not," Charlie reassured her. "Trust me, if this was a regular day, I'd be doing back-breaking labor for the next eight hours. This is kind of like a vacation." She caught the look Luma shot her and amended, "Well, not for you, obviously. Sorry."

"It's okay," Luma said.

"Will you come outside with me?" Charlie asked. "I want to show you something."

Luma glanced at the towering pile of laundry, but the washing machine hadn't even reached its first spin cycle and it would be a while before they got through all of that. She nodded and Charlie grabbed a cardboard box from a set of them stacked near the door.

Luma paused in the doorway and Charlie looked back at her. "Scared?"

"No," Luma said. "It's just that I'm going to ruin your slippers wearing them outside."

Charlie laughed. "They've survived worse than a little dirt. Come on."

So Luma came into the swept yard and followed Charlie around the side of the cottage. The sun was shining brightly and it felt welcome and warm on her bare arms, the wind rustling through her skirt. Before she knew it, Luma was smiling despite all her troubles.

"It's so peaceful out here," she said. "No traffic, nothing but the birds singing."

Charlie looked into the trees surrounding the cottage, as if she hadn't noticed them before, then said, "It's a-"

"Cuckoo," Luma said in unison with her. "I know – I had to learn birdsongs in my middle school biology class."

"Very good," Charlie said, smiling. They came to a stop outside the large brick fireplace and Charlie set the box down in front of it. "Do you know what this is?"

"Yes," Luma said. "It's my North Star."

"Huh?"

"There was a fire in it the day I got here," she explained. "I saw the smoke and it led me to the cottage. If it wasn't for that, I'd probably still be wandering the forest."

Charlie smiled and said, "Glad I could be of service. This is my pottery kiln."

"Then I have you to thank for my life," Luma said, looking into Charlie's gemstone eyes.

Charlie opened the steel door and they both leaned down to look inside. There were a couple of rows of shelving and about a dozen clay vases fired in a rainbow of pretty colors sat on the shelves.

"I normally fire new pieces during the day, leave

them to cool overnight and then pack them up in the morning," Charlie explained, reaching into the kiln and carefully extracting a vase. "But I forgot about these vases with everything else going on."

She wrapped the first one in butcher paper that was waiting for her inside the box. Then she laid it in the bottom of the box and reached for another vase.

"Here," Luma said, picking up a piece of butcher paper and holding her hand out for the vase. "You retrieve, I'll wrap."

Charlie handed her the vase and Luma inspected it for a moment. Each one had its own unique design etched into the clay – flowers, leaves, filigrees and geometric shapes. Luma took great care with the butcher paper, saying, "Charlie, these are beautiful. You made them?"

"Yeah," she said, keeping her eyes fixed on the kiln. "It was just a hobby when I was a kid, but it turns out I have a knack for it and people are willing to buy my pottery."

"Where do you sell them?"

"There's a nursery in Grimm Falls whose customers took a liking to the vases," Charlie said. "I keep the nursery stocked with a small display of them and the owner told me last week that she was running low, so I fired up this batch for her. Other than that, I take special orders from time to time, but the lumber-jack business takes up my days, so it's mostly just for fun."

"I think you could turn this into a real business if you wanted," Luma said. "Sell them outside of Grimm Falls."

"Someday, I hope," Charlie said with a bashful smile. They finished packing the vases up and Charlie carried the box back to the cottage. As they walked, she said, "I promised I'd drop these off in town this week. If you're up for it, you can come with me and we'll get you some shoes."

"Maybe," Luma said, although the idea made her stomach tremble with butterflies.

———

They went back into the cottage and Luma kept an eye on the washing machine, making sure to get all the sets of sheets washed and dried before Charlie's brothers came back from the forest. Charlie helped her make each bed, and she refused to back down when Luma tried to give her little twin bed back to her at bedtime.

That night, Luma slept in Charlie's bed again, and Charlie insisted on taking the couch.

Luma dreamed about her mom again, but this time when her mother was supposed to show up and save her from Tabitha, nothing happened. Tabitha just kept coming, marching toward Luma like a horror movie villain, and Luma curled into a ball on the floor. She was waiting for Tabitha to kill her, and when nothing happened, Luma peeked over her knees to see Charlie charging at Tabitha with an ax. She scared Tabitha off, then pulled Luma to her feet and wrapped her free arm around Luma's waist.

My hero, dream-Luma said, looking into Charlie's gorgeous aquamarine eyes. Her scar was gone, and along with it, the self-consciousness with which she was forever adjusting her hair over her forehead. Her arms were strong from so much time swinging that ax, and she smelled piney like the forest, a scent that made Luma want to sink against her.

Luma awoke to the dawn chorus of a couple of robins outside the window. The sky was just beginning to lighten with the onset of a new day and Luma was feeling a little more hopeful than the day before. She stretched, put her feet into Charlie's soft slippers, then went into the common area.

Charlie was sleeping soundly on the couch, the last embers of the night's fire still burning in the hearth. Luma thought about waking her, but she looked peaceful so instead, she padded into the kitchen and quietly pulled open the refrigerator door.

The first couple of mornings in the cottage had been absolute chaos with six people all trying to get ready for work, and Luma just trying to stay out of everyone's way. She figured the least she could do was give herself a purpose.

She found a dozen eggs in a carton and a big, heavy pack of meat in butcher paper that she unwrapped to reveal sausage links. She and Charlie had washed and put away all the dishes from the previous days' meals, so Luma already knew her way around the kitchen fairly well. She retrieved a large pan from the lower cabinets and started cooking.

She cooked the sausages first, glancing over at the couch every so often to see if the sizzle of the meat would wake Charlie up, or the smell permeating the cottage. Charlie slept on, though, and Luma finished with the sausages, piling them high on a serving tray and moving it to the dining table. She moved on to the eggs, draining the sausage grease and cooking them in batches in the same pan.

Scotty was the first to emerge from the master bedroom, sliding on his glasses as he crossed over to the kitchen. He smiled broadly and said, "Smells great in here."

"I found some sausage links in the fridge – I hope it's okay that I used them all," Luma said.

"Okay? It's great," Scotty said. He paused at the table to take a sausage link and bit into it, then groaned his appreciation. "Let me tell you, you did that sausage more justice than Maxwell usually can. He cooks out of necessity and we appreciate it, but he's not exactly a chef. This, on the other hand... delicious."

"Thank you," Luma said, beaming. "I picked up a few things from watching my dad's personal chef do her magic."

So relatable, she chastised herself, but Scotty didn't

seem to notice. A few of the other brothers came out of their bedrooms, some heading straight for the plate of sausage while the others stood in the hall, vying for their turn in the bathroom.

Luma looked toward the couch, and Charlie was still asleep. Amused, she went over and crouched down in front of her.

"Hey," she whispered, then nudged Charlie's shoulder when she didn't stir.

Finally, her eyes fluttered open. "Hmm?"

An adorable, sleepy smile spread across her lips as she saw who was waking her, an honest moment between sleep and full wakefulness. It sent a warm sensation between Luma's thighs as she remembered her dream and her eyes lingered over Charlie's biceps, wondering how they would feel wrapped around her.

"I made breakfast," Luma said. "You're not going to get any if you don't hurry. Your brothers have some appetite."

"They really do," Charlie said, sitting up and wiping the sleep from her eyes. "Thanks."

Then her hand went to her bangs and smoothed them over her forehead. Luma wanted to tell her that her birthmark wasn't off-putting like she obviously believed it was. If anything, she thought it might be shaped like a heart, but she couldn't tell for sure because she never got a very good look at it.

"You sleep like a log," Luma teased as Charlie got

up. "I was worried I would wake you when I started cooking."

"Six brothers," Charlie said, nodding toward the table, where all of the Jacobs boys were now hovering around the sausage plate like vultures instead of sitting to eat a civilized meal.

"Right," Luma said with a smile. She went over to the kitchen island and grabbed a stack of earthenware plates – Charlie's handiwork, she now realized. She set them down on the table, then carried a couple serving plates full of fluffy scrambled eggs over and said, "Sit down everyone. You can't start the work day off with a stomach ache from eating standing up."

They all obeyed her request, and Luma glanced over at Charlie, who was giving her an amused look. She smiled back, then held out a plate for her.

"Will you stay with me again today?" She asked when Charlie had filled her plate and sat down to eat.

"Of course," Charlie said, those aquamarines sparkling in the morning sun.

7

CHARLIE

Charlie convinced Luma to go into town with her that day after her brothers left to finish the Wilson lumber order.

"I have to go regardless," she said. "Green Thumb's going to want their vases, and I hate the idea of leaving you alone here."

"I'm sure Antonio doesn't know where I am," Luma said. "But I really could use a change of clothes."

She'd borrowed Charlie's bathrobe yesterday and put her clothes in the washing machine along with the final load of sheets, and the idea of Luma's naked body inside Charlie's robe was something that had proved rather distracting for the rest of the day. Still, there were only so many days she could keep washing and wearing the same clothes – a thigh-grazing skirt and a thin blouse that weren't the most appropriate choices for forest life.

"Come on, then," Charlie said. "We'll go into Grimm Falls, I'll drop off my order of vases, and then I'll take you shopping. You look ridiculous in those slippers."

Luma laughed and said, "I don't have my wallet. All I've got is the clothes on my back."

"We'll fill out an IOU," Charlie said.

"Thank you," Luma said. "Seriously – you're being so nice to me when you could have just kicked me out."

Charlie subtly shook her head to arrange her bangs and said, "You're pretty nice yourself. Are we going into town or not?"

"Yeah," Luma said. "Let's go."

Charlie nodded to a pair of work boots sitting neatly by the door. She was wearing the sneakers that she liked when she wasn't working, and the steel-toed boots were the only other ones she could offer Luma. "They're a little big for you, but they beat wearing slippers into town."

Luma sat down at the dinner table to put them on. She was already wearing a pair of Charlie's socks, and as she slipped her small feet into the work boots, Charlie cringed.

They were dirty, their toes scuffed and the laces fraying after a month of rugged wear, and Charlie hated the thought of Luma having to endure them. She carefully laced up the boots. Charlie never bothered with her laces – she just shoved her heels into her shoes and went, but it was cute how much care Luma was taking with them.

When Luma stood and their eyes met again, she said, "I'm lucky you're here – I wouldn't be able to borrow any of your brothers' shoes."

Charlie snorted at the image – Luma walking like a toddler in enormous shoes that threatened to fall off with every step. Their eyes lingered on each other, then Charlie headed over to the door and picked up the full box. She balanced it on her shoulder and opened the cottage door.

Luma slipped past her, the hem of her skirt brushing against Charlie's jeans. Her pure black hair shone in the sunlight and she had an optimistic bounce to her step in spite of everything.

Charlie had just met this girl four days ago and yet she had a strange urge to please her, to protect her, to make her smile and brighten her day. She pointed Luma around the corner of the cottage to a car port housing the family pickup truck. Charlie strapped the cardboard box into the truck bed while Luma got into the passenger seat, then she slid in beside her.

The truck cabin had never felt so small and Charlie tried not to glance across the bench seat at Luma as she turned the key in the ignition and they bounced slowly along a dirt path out to the road that would take them to Grimm Falls.

"We better get your new shoes first," Charlie said, hazarding a glance at the footwell where Luma's feet were swimming in her work boots. "I don't want you to trip in those things."

"Whatever you want," Luma said. "I'm just along for the ride."

No, you've got that backward, honey, Charlie thought.

―――――

When they got into town, Charlie parked the truck on Main Street in front of her favorite thrift store. She killed the engine and asked, "Is second-hand okay? This is where I do most of my shopping."

"Fine by me," Luma said. Then she caught the way that Charlie was looking at her and asked, "What?"

"You don't look like a thrift store kind of girl," Charlie said. "Grimm Falls is somewhat limited in our clothing options. There's a boutique two streets over, though. We could-"

"No," Luma laughed, putting her hand on Charlie's forearm and freezing the words in her mouth. "I don't want you to go out of your way for me. I'll be happy with any pair of shoes that have thick soles after all the pine needles I've stepped in."

Charlie reached for her door handle, but Luma didn't move yet.

"Are you nervous?" Charlie asked.

"A little," Luma admitted. "I'm sure Antonio caught the first cab or Uber he could back to Rockledge, but I still feel a little... *exposed* here. The forest was more comforting."

Charlie smiled. "I think so, too. But don't worry – you're safe with me."

Luma flashed her a smile, then got out of the truck. They met on the sidewalk and went inside the thrift store. Charlie pointed Luma toward the women's clothing racks, then hung around the cash register to give her space. She chatted with the cashier – a girl she went to high school with – and snuck surreptitious glances at Luma as she flipped through the racks, inspecting the price tags on everything.

Luma disappeared into the shop's only dressing room after a few minutes, then emerged with a couple of items draped over her arms. She was wearing a vintage band t-shirt and a pair of acid washed jeans that were surprisingly stylish, or maybe that was just the effect Luma had on all clothes.

Charlie's mouth dropped involuntarily for a moment before she shut it again. She'd been sure that Luma was the most beautiful woman she'd ever seen from the moment she laid eyes on her... but she somehow managed to become even more appealing in jeans and a t-shirt. She'd transformed into a girl next door, still intimidatingly beautiful but now Charlie could imagine she was not *completely* out of her league.

In some universe, at least.

In this one, she was still untouchable.

"Well?" she asked. "How do I look?"

"You, uh, you're..." Charlie stuttered. If she'd said what was on her mind, it would have come out sounding an awful lot like *ahoogah*.

The girl behind the counter laughed and answered with ease, "*Love* that vintage tee. You should definitely get it."

"It's thirty-five dollars altogether," Luma said apologetically. "The sneakers were the most expensive."

Charlie looked down at her feet, noticing for the first time that she was wearing a pair of red cross-trainers that somehow perfectly completed the look.

"Don't worry about the price," Charlie said. "You should pick out some more clothes, though, so you don't have to wear the same thing every day. Unless you're planning on leaving soon?"

She wasn't sure what answer she was hoping for. On one hand, she was really enjoying Luma's company – and the view. On the other hand, there was no way in hell she was going to accomplish what she wanted in the forest with Luma around. How could Charlie forget about women when the most beautiful one she'd ever seen was sleeping in her bed and borrowing her robe?

Luma glanced at the cashier, then told Charlie, "I can't leave yet. I'll go find a couple more cheap things – thanks."

She left Charlie's boots on the counter, along with

a small bundle of her old clothes, then she disappeared into the racks. A small wave of relief washed over Charlie - whatever her conscious mind wanted, her heart clearly wasn't done with this girl yet.

Luma came back a minute or two later with a couple more shirts, another pair of jeans, a pair of pajamas, a gray hoodie, and a new pack of plain white briefs tucked discretely into the middle of the pile. She looked sheepish as she set it all down on the counter and asked Charlie once again, "Is this too much?"

"Buy whatever you need," Charlie assured her.

"Is it okay if I wear these out of the store?" Luma asked the cashier. The girl nodded and Luma pulled the tags off of what she was wearing so the girl could ring them up. They watched the bill tally up and as Charlie paid, Luma nudged her with her shoulder. "Thank you. I'll pay you back for all of this – I promise."

They left the thrift store and put Luma's new clothes in the truck, then Charlie got her vases out of the back and they headed across the street to Green Thumb Nursery.

As they walked, Luma let out a satisfied moan and said, "I really appreciate you lending me your shoes, but man, it feels good to wear the right size again."

"I bet," Charlie said.

She pushed the door to the nursery open and a little bell above the door jingled. There were plants, gardening tools and bags of soil arranged all over the front of the shop, with a long greenhouse extending off the back of the building. For a weekday, there were a lot of people in the shop getting their gardens ready for summer.

Charlie led Luma to the cash register and they waited in line behind a woman buying a potted orchid, then she set her box down on the counter. The woman standing behind the register looked to be in her early forties, with tightly curled hair and a daisy tucked behind her ear.

"Hi, Amelie," Charlie said. "I've got that order of vases you wanted."

"Oh, great," she said, digging right into the box and carefully unwrapping one of them. "Beautiful as always, Charlie." Then she caught sight of Luma standing just behind Charlie and said with a wink, "Speaking of beautiful… who's your friend?"

Charlie looked back at Luma, who shook her head. The poor girl was still nervous about being in town, so Charlie deflected attention away from her. "She's just visiting for a little while, agreed to tag along on my errands. So, how did people like the different colored glazes on the last set of vases I brought in?"

"They loved them," Amelie said. She pointed to the front of the shop, where a nearly empty display shelf stood by the door. "I moved them to the window because I figured they'd be eye-catching and bring people inside. You can see by how empty the shelf is that it worked."

"Great," Charlie said, beaming with pride. While she was looking, she noticed two more people had gotten in line behind them. "Well, I can save you a little labor and put out the new ones myself if you like."

"Would you?" Amelie asked. "Oh, that would be great – we're so busy in the spring."

She opened the cash register and gave Charlie a pre-written check, her cut of the sales from the last set of vases. Then Charlie stepped aside, taking her cardboard box and leading Luma over to the display shelf. Luma helped her unpack the new ones and as they worked, she kept smiling at Charlie.

"What?" she asked.

"You're kind of a big deal," Luma said.

"I am not," Charlie said, blushing.

"You are," Luma said. "I think it's really cool. What got you into pottery?"

"I've always loved it," Charlie said. "I love using my hands to shape something that came from the earth."

She trailed off as she noticed Luma biting her lower lip. Was that desire she saw? Charlie swallowed hard and turned her focus back to her vase display. Was *she* the reason for that look in Luma's eyes? Had *her* words had that effect on her?

It certainly seemed like it.

"I've never known what I want to do when I grow up," Luma said. "Modeling's the only thing that's ever jumped out at me, but my heart's not in it."

"You'll figure it out," Charlie said. "I'm sure you've got the world in your hands." Luma rolled her eyes – Charlie had struck a nerve. "I'm sorry. Did I say something wrong?"

"No," Luma said. "You're right - I've basically had my life handed to me, and yet I haven't even figured out what I want yet."

"What about the modeling contract?" Charlie asked.

Luma shrugged. "I could do it, but I don't have a passion for it—that's Tabitha's dream. I want to be more than just a pretty face, but maybe that's all I have to offer."

"I've only known you a few days and I can already tell that's not true," Charlie said. They finished the display and Charlie waved goodbye to Amelie, then the two of them headed back onto the street.

As Charlie was strapping the empty box back into the truck bed so it wouldn't fly away on the way home, Luma looked up Main Street and asked, "Is that a public library?"

"Yeah," Charlie said, following her gaze to a little brick building on the corner. "Do you want to go in?"

Luma paused a moment, then said, "No. They have computers there, though, right?"

Charlie laughed. "Grimm Falls is a small town, but this *is* the twenty-first century. Why do you ask?"

"I think when the time's right, it would be safe to

email my dad," Luma said. Then she frowned and said, "But I have no idea when the time's going to be right."

"Hey, I have an idea," Charlie said, trying to lift Luma's spirits. "Do you mind sticking around town for a little bit longer?"

"Okay," Luma said. "What do you have in mind?"

Charlie pointed up the street in the other direction. "Want to get a cup of coffee?"

———

The Magic Bean was a quaint little coffee shop with two levels of seating, upstairs and down. Charlie led Luma up to the counter, explaining that the cafe was a staple for Grimm Falls College students and she'd become somewhat addicted to it during her year at the school.

"Do you miss college?" Luma asked.

"Not really," Charlie said. "I did well in high school so everyone just assumed I would go to college, but I prefer to be outdoors, not sitting in a classroom. What about you - were you going to go to college before all of this?"

"No," Luma said. "I was planning to take a gap year - my dad thought it would be a good idea for me to do some traveling—see the world and find out if that sparks any realizations about what I should be doing with my life."

Luma ordered a peppermint tea and Charlie got

her favorite, a toffee nut flavored coffee. The owner of the cafe, Rhonda, came up to the counter when she spotted Charlie and said hello, then handed her an envelope, smiling broadly.

"I finally got a chance to talk to the interior designers," she said. "We're going ahead with the project - the details are in there."

"Great," Charlie said, slipping the envelope into her back pocket. "I'll get started right away."

She was trying to be casual about the whole thing so Luma wouldn't ask too many questions. If she had to tell her about the project, Charlie figured she'd end up even redder than she was when Luma called her a big deal in the nursery.

They got their drinks and Charlie led Luma upstairs to the loft. It was cozy up there, with tables and plush chairs arranged around a U-shaped balcony that overlooked the rest of the cafe. It wasn't too busy in the middle of the afternoon, and all the other patrons were sitting on the lower level so Charlie and Luma had the loft to themselves.

They settled into a pair of armchairs and Luma inhaled with a covetous smile when she caught a waft of Charlie's coffee. Charlie noticed and laughed. "Do you want to try it?"

"Just a sip?" Luma asked.

Charlie handed the coffee over and Luma took a long drink. The coffee was buttery, Charlie's favorite, and watching the divine smile that pasted itself across

Luma's lips ended up being better than the coffee itself.

"That good?" Charlie asked. She didn't quite meet Luma's eyes when she asked.

"Yeah," Luma said, trying to hand the coffee back.

Charlie refused to take it, saying, "I've had about a hundred cups of The Magic Bean's toffee nut brew. I'll trade you."

"Really?" Luma asked.

"Yeah," Charlie said, reaching for her peppermint tea.

Luma gave it to her, then said, "So, are you going to tell me about the top-secret envelope in your back pocket or not?"

Charlie smiled, then said, "I was hoping you would forget about that."

"Oh, now I have to know," Luma prodded, her eyes going bright with intrigue. "Does it involve your pottery business?"

"Yeah," Charlie said, pulling the envelope out of her pocket. "Rhonda wants to give The Magic Bean a makeover. She's been working with an interior decorator, but she said she wanted me to make her some custom mugs to add a little local flavor to the finished look. I've been waiting on her to get with the designer and tell me whether the project is going ahead."

She opened the envelope and unfolded the paper inside for Luma to see. It had color swatches and a reference image of the cafe's logo for Charlie to use. When she looked back at Luma, she was beaming.

"That's incredible!" She said. "Does that mean it's time to start making mugs?"

"Yeah, big time," Charlie said with a laugh. "I have to make about twelve dozen of them."

Luma bit her lip and Charlie nearly fell out of her chair when she asked, "Can I watch?"

Charlie swallowed hard. "You want to?"

"Yeah," Luma said. "I'm curious."

"Sure," Charlie said, her voice sounding huskier than she expected.

She'd already told her parents and her brothers about the pending deal when Rhonda first mentioned it a couple of months ago. They had all been just as enthusiastic and proud as Luma was, although her parents were also nervous since it had played a small role in her decision not to go back to school in the fall. But somehow, Luma's admiration was just as important to Charlie as her own family's.

"So, do you think that coffee will taste better in a Charlie Jacobs mug?" She asked, gesturing to the ordinary take-out cup that Luma held in her hand.

"Without a doubt," Luma said. She wrinkled her nose in that adorable way she had and added, "Although I'll have to taste it for myself just to be sure."

8

LUMA

A few days later, Luma was washing the dishes after dinner and Charlie's brothers were lounging on the couches while Thomas built a fire. Charlie disappeared for a little while right after dinner and just as Luma was grabbing a towel to start drying the dishes, she looked out the window to see Charlie coming up the path.

The sky was nearly dark and she was little more than a silhouette, but Luma could tell that Charlie's hands were caked with mud, and she had a metal bucket slung over one arm. Curious, Luma left the dishes and went outside. She laughed when she got closer and saw just how filthy Charlie was. Her forearms were covered nearly up to her elbows and the knees of her jeans were just as dirty and wet.

"What have you been up to?" She asked, shaking her head.

"The clay doesn't dig itself up," Charlie said, walking into the clearing around the cottage. She headed for the woodshed and Luma followed her.

She peeked into the bucket slung over Charlie's arm - it was half-full of rich red clay, and upon closer inspection, she noticed that was what Charlie had all over her hands - clay, not mud. "Where do you get the clay?"

"Anywhere I feel like digging," Charlie said. "The whole forest is clay once you get about ten inches below the surface."

She opened the shed and used a towel hanging there to wipe off a small hand trowel she retrieved from the bucket, then she hung the trowel on a hook. She glanced at Luma and laughed.

"What?" Luma asked.

"You act like this is the most fascinating thing you've ever seen," Charlie said. "It's just clay."

"I've never dug raw materials out of the ground," Luma said. "Look at me – I've never even spent this much time outside before I came here."

Charlie smiled and said, "Well, it suits you." Her eyes glanced over Luma's body momentarily and then she averted her gaze again. "I was going to save you the boredom of watching me get everything set up, but since you're here... do you still want to watch me work?"

Luma nodded and a little shiver of desire worked its way unexpectedly through her at the image of

Charlie working with the clay. *Now that you mentioned it, yes, I really do want to watch you mold lumps of cool clay into something beautiful with your bare hands.*

Luma bit her lip and Charlie looked away.

"We'll take everything out in the open so we have some light to see by. Can you grab that lantern?" Charlie nodded to one hanging from a hook inside the small shed and Luma picked it up, then closed the door and followed Charlie around the side of the cottage.

As they went, Luma was vaguely aware of eyes on them – six sets, she was guessing, from the living room windows. All of Charlie's brothers had taken note of how much she was monopolizing Luma's attention, and one by one, they were getting the picture.

Adam seemed like the only one who hadn't figured out yet that Luma was interested in Charlie... well, besides Charlie herself.

Luma ignored their audience until they rounded the corner of the cottage, out of view of the living room windows. Charlie was oblivious to the whole thing and she set the bucket down, then went to a spigot on the side of the cottage and used it to wash the clay from her hands. When they were clean, she filled another bucket with water and retrieved a wooden stool – hand carved like everything else around here. She set the bucket and stool down beside the kiln.

"That's for you," Charlie said, gesturing to the stool. "I'll be right back."

"Thanks," Luma answered. Charlie disappeared around the side of the cottage again, then returned a moment later carrying an awkwardly-shaped table that Luma surmised was a pottery wheel.

She set it down about a foot from Luma's stool, giving her a front-row seat to watch Charlie work. There was a seat built into the table, a spinning disk a little larger than a dinner plate formed the work surface where the clay would go, and there was a foot pedal to turn it.

Charlie lit the lantern and placed it on top of the kiln to illuminate the area. It was dusk and it would be full dark soon, but for now, the lantern provided enough light. As she sat down, Luma asked, "Are you going to start on your cafe order?"

"Yep, it's going to be all mugs, all the time for a while," Charlie said. "So I'm afraid you'll get bored pretty quick."

"Impossible," Luma said. "Have you ever gotten a big order before?"

"No," Charlie said, and even in the flickering light of the lantern, Luma could see her swelling with pride. "Now everybody who gets a cup of coffee at The Magic Bean is going to be drinking out of one of my creations."

Luma couldn't take her eyes off of Charlie's blue-green gaze. She held it, too, and for the first time since they'd met, Charlie seemed oblivious to the fact that her bangs had been swept to the side in the effort of hauling the pottery wheel outside.

The pink outline of her scar was visible and although Luma was curious about the thing Charlie spent so much time trying to hide, she didn't want to pry. Charlie caught her looking, though, so Luma asked, "That's a birthmark, right?"

"It used to be," she said. "In most kids, they go away on their own but for me, it was interfering with my vision and the doctors had to treat it with a laser when I was about two years old. What's left the scar from the laser, and I've got that for life."

Luma reached across the space between them, ready to take her hand away if Charlie flinched, but she allowed Luma to push her bangs behind her ears. The mark was large and pink, and Luma had the opportunity to really look at it for the first time in the lantern light. It covered Charlie's forehead and her left eyelid, and Charlie wouldn't look at Luma while she was touching her face.

"You're self-conscious, but you don't need to be," Luma said, letting Charlie's bangs fall back across her face. "You're a very attractive girl." Charlie snorted at her and Luma said, "Really. I mean it."

"*You* think *I'm* attractive?" Charlie repeated, arching an eyebrow at her.

"Is that so hard to believe?" Luma asked.

"Yes," Charlie said. It always came back to Luma's appearance, and she hated that. People in Rockledge thought she was pretty so they could treat her like an object to be lusted after, and Charlie thought she was too pretty to be interested in her.

"Well, then, I guess I'll just have to convince you," Luma said.

Charlie looked away, clearing her throat as she dipped her hand into the bucket of clay. She slapped a handful of it onto the wheel and Luma let out a surprised shriek as a few flecks of it sprayed every-where, including the front of her shirt and a little dot of it on Charlie's cheek.

"Sorry," she said.

"It's okay," Luma answered quickly. She picked off the little bit of clay on her t-shirt, trying to be as nonchalant about it as possible because the last thing she wanted right then was for Charlie to decide she was a prissy city girl who never got dirty... even though she was a prissy city girl who never got dirty.

"Here," Charlie said, reaching across the wheel with her clean hand. "There's some in your hair."

She ran her fingers through Luma's hair and her heart didn't beat at all. Something powerful came over her every time Charlie came near, and it was gaining speed with every look and touch. Charlie's fingers didn't linger long. She did an efficient job of isolating the little bit of clay that had speckled Luma's hair, and then she was drawing back again.

And Luma's heart was beating again.

"Thanks," she said.

"No problem."

"You, uh-" she started to point out the clay on Charlie's cheek. Some part of her badly wanted to return the gesture, to take it one step further and actually caress the softness of her cheek... but that part of her was small and it chickened out. So she pantomimed the problem on her own cheek and said, "You have a little bit of clay, too."

Charlie didn't bother wiping it off. She just grinned and said, "Hazard of the job."

Then she dipped her hands into the bucket of water and cupped both hands around the little ball of clay in the center of the wheel. She started to pedal and Luma watched, mesmerized, as Charlie used her palms to shape the clay, rewetting her hands periodically and pressing her thumbs down into the center of the ball to form the inside of the cup. She made it look effortless as she drew the excess clay upward to shape the rim. It was amazing how quickly it went from a hunk of earth to an actual coffee mug, smooth and pleasing to the eye.

Charlie stopped pedaling and Luma's astonishment must have been written all over her face because Charlie laughed at her. "Haven't you ever played with clay before? You must have had a fancy art class when you were in school."

"Sure," Luma said. "But that was elementary school, and what I made was more like lumpy stick figure dogs. Not something beautiful like that. Charlie, you have a gift."

She reached into the bucket and pulled out a small lump of clay about the size of a quarter. She ignored Luma's compliment as she rolled the clay out to a snake-like shape, then formed it against the side of the cup, using her fingers to turn it into a handle and dabbing on a little more water to fix it in place.

"It just takes practice," she said, taking a long, thin wire from where it had been tucked along the edge of the table and separating the cup from the wheel. She carried it carefully over to the kiln and Luma jumped up to open the door for her. Charlie put the mug on one of the shelves and said, "There - one down, a hundred and forty-three to go. I'll make a dozen tonight and let them air-dry overnight, then paint and fire the first batch tomorrow. Should be able to get through the order in about two weeks at that pace."

"When's it due?" Luma asked.

"Rhonda's remodel won't happen for another couple of months so I've got lots of time," Charlie said. She hooked her clay-covered thumb toward the house. "I knew I'd need it with brothers like those—you never know what's going to come up."

Luma smiled and added, "And house guests like me."

"You're no trouble," Charlie said.

"In that case," Luma answered, trailing off.

"What?" Charlie asked, one eyebrow quirking.

"Can I give it the proverbial spin?" Luma asked, gesturing to the pottery wheel.

"Really?" Charlie asked.

"Yeah," Luma said, growing brazen and going over to the table. She sat down and put her hands on her hips. "I can get dirty too, you know."

"I'm sure you can," Charlie said, and as they both registered the innuendo in those words, she went over to the clay bucket and dropped a baseball-sized lump into the center of the wheel, careful not to splash Luma this time. Then she said, "Knock yourself out."

Luma started pedaling and the clay tumbled out to the edge of the wheel. She yelped and Charlie put her hand out to catch it just before it flew off the table entirely. Luma took her foot off the pedal and the wheel slowed to a stop.

Charlie looked at her, amusement in her eyes as she plopped the clay back onto the center of the wheel and said, "You have to wet your hands and cup the clay, then pedal, or else that happens."

"Oh," Luma said. She did as Charlie instructed, dipping her hands into the chilly water and cupping them around the clay. Then she started to work the pedal again. Charlie stood beside her, ready to intervene if she got in trouble again.

The clay was cool like the earth and it squelched and oozed between her fingers when she applied pressure to it. She was building a tiny, wobbly clay tower that soon rose above the height of her hands and started to get away from her.

"Put your thumbs on top of it," Charlie said. "You control the shape – make it do what you want."

There was that shiver of desire again at Charlie's commanding words. *If only I had that much power...* As the tower of clay began to droop over Luma's hands, becoming messy and misshapen, she said, "You're giving me too much credit. The clay obviously has the upper hand here."

Charlie laughed, and then her hands were on top of Luma's. She knelt beside her in the dirt, their shoulders pressed together as she guided Luma's hands through the clay.

Luma hardly noticed the fact that her out of control lump of clay was beginning to take shape again. All she was focused on was the way Charlie's hands felt over hers, and how slippery everything was getting as hot hands mixed with cold, wet clay.

It was a very appealing sensation.

"Now push your thumbs down," Charlie said. Her thumbs applied pressure on top of Luma's and they plunged into the clay.

"Whoa," Luma said as the lump suddenly took a different form entirely. Just like that, it was a cup. A short, squatty cup that would be very awkward to hold, but still – it was something that hadn't existed just a second ago. "That's incredible."

"Mm-hmm," Charlie said. Her attention was fixed

on using Luma's hands to form the cup and she was oblivious to the way the vibration of her words – so close to Luma's ears – was affecting her. She couldn't, or else she'd be having just as much trouble focusing on the clay as Luma was.

Charlie shaped Luma's hands into pincers, pointing straight down at the wheel and slowly guiding the clay upward to form the walls of the cup. Her hands stayed close to Luma's, giving her gentle directions and laying over hers whenever she needed more help. It wasn't until Charlie told her to stop pedaling that it seemed like their physical proximity occurred to her.

She looked at Luma and in the glow of the lantern, her aquamarine eyes were like gemstones again. All the facets glimmered and lit something in Luma's belly, and then she was twisting around, her legs getting tangled in the pottery wheel as she brought her hands to Charlie's face and kissed her.

Luma's eyes closed, she felt the heat of Charlie's body so close to her own, and she wondered if what she was doing was crazy. Then Charlie's arm circled around Luma's waist, pulling her hungrily toward her. Luma parted her lips and Charlie's tongue rushed to fill the space, slick and warm just like the clay. Luma let out an involuntary moan and Charlie sank against her.

I knew it. You want me.

Then Luma felt herself losing balance, one of the

pottery wheel's legs lifting off the ground. Her eyes flew open and she let out a little yelp just in time for Charlie to release her from the kiss and brace her, keeping her from falling to the ground.

"Whoa," Charlie said, and Luma wasn't sure if that was in response to the kiss, or the near-toppling of her pottery wheel.

"Yeah," Luma said. She laughed and added, "I got clay all over your cheeks. I'm sorry."

"Don't be," Charlie said and Luma wanted to laugh, but she was afraid Charlie's self-conscious streak would come back. She loved feeling it dissolve as their bodies pressed together.

Charlie put her hands into the water bucket and used it to clean her face, and while she did, she stole a glance at Luma. "Well, I guess I don't have to worry anymore that you're into my brothers."

This time, Luma did laugh. "No. Your brothers are great, but none of them are my type."

"And I am?" Charlie asked, incredulous.

"Why not?" Luma challenged. "You don't give yourself enough credit."

"We better finish before it's pitch-black out here," Charlie said.

"Okay," Luma answered. "I'll get out of your way. We can just throw my mug back into the bucket—no need to waste clay."

"It's not a waste," Charlie said. "It's a good mug, and you have to finish it." She pulled the stool over and sat down again, reaching into the bucket for a small hunk of clay to form the handle. "Here – last step."

She put the little piece of clay on the edge of the wheel for Luma and she picked it up, rolling it back and forth between her palms like she'd seen Charlie do with the last handle. The mug was thin on one side and a little bit lopsided, like something you might see at the Mad Hatter's tea party. "You're not actually going to give that to Rhonda, are you?"

Charlie shrugged. "We'll see how it fires up. If the quality isn't up to snuff, you can take it home as a souvenir."

Luma rolled the clay meticulously through her palms until Charlie grabbed her wrist and laughed.

"That's thin enough," she said. "It's gonna break in the kiln if you make it much smaller."

"Here," Luma said, trying to hand it to her. "You put it on the cup."

"Nope," Charlie said, "This is your creation. You do it."

Luma did, and she couldn't say that it looked good, but if she squinted, it did resemble a coffee mug. She felt strangely proud as she watched Charlie separate it from the wheel and carry it to the kiln. She set it inside, then Luma took her seat back on the spectator's stool. Charlie sat down and tossed another ball of clay onto the wheel, then said, "By the way, my brothers and I always go into town to eat lunch with our parents once a week. We're going tomorrow—do you want to come?"

"To meet the parents?" Luma asked, smiling. Charlie had a goofy grin on her face and Luma wondered if it was too soon to kiss her again. She decided to let Charlie initiate the next time and said, "I'd love to meet them."

"Good," Charlie said. "It's a date."

Then she banged out ten more cups in a little more time than it had taken the two of them to make one, and transferred them all to the kiln. She left the door open to allow for air flow that would dry the clay, and Luma helped her put away the supplies.

Just before they went back into the cottage, Charlie took Luma's hand and they lingered in the dark. Luma could feel her body close, swaying nearer and then hesitating and backing away. *Does she want to kiss me again?*

She hoped for it, but instead, Charlie asked, "Did you mean what you said about me being attractive?"

"Of course," Luma breathed.

Charlie seemed a little deflated—definitely not the reaction Luma was expecting. "How can every other girl in my life be repulsed by my scar, and yet you're the one that's different? I'm having a hard time wrapping my head around it."

"Well," Luma said, stepping a little closer to Charlie, "Obviously, all the other girls in your life sucked. I think you're hot, scar and all."

Charlie laughed, but it didn't quite reach her eyes. "It figures—the only girl that can see past my scar belongs to a completely different world and is destined to leave me, sooner rather than later."

Luma slipped her hand into Charlie's. "I like you. I think you like me, too. Neither of us can know what's going to happen, but it might be fun to find out. Don't you think?"

"Yes," Charlie said. Luma trailed her hand up Charlie's arm, feeling the definition of her strong arms as she tilted her head slightly up to meet Charlie's lips.

Then the cottage door opened, throwing light across the yard as Scotty called, "Did you two get eaten by a bear or what?"

Luma laughed, half amused and half frustrated at having been denied a second kiss. Then Charlie took her hand and they went to the door. As they walked past Scotty into the cottage, she held her head high and said, "No bear would dare mess with me."

9

CHARLIE

On Saturday, everyone spread out around the cottage to relax. Thomas, Maxwell and Joey played video games in the living room, Braden stayed in bed all morning to catch up on his sleep, and Scotty and Adam were entrenched in a lively game of War at the dinner table. Charlie and Luma were outside, taking a completed batch of mugs for The Magic Bean out of the kiln.

When it was time to head into town and meet Charlie's parents for lunch, Adam led the charge out of the house, spinning the truck keys on his finger as he called, "Come on, gang, it's time to go!"

"You ready for this?" Charlie asked Luma.

"Why not?" Luma asked with a laugh.

Five of the brothers squeezed into the truck bed and that left Luma, Charlie and Adam to share the bench seat. Adam took the wheel, Luma sat in the middle and Charlie sat beside her.

She thought the cabin of the truck had felt narrow when it was just the two of them and they went into town the first time, but now, Charlie's hips touched Luma's and their bodies jostled against each other with every bump and tree root on the path out to the road. On Luma's other side, Adam was mashed up against her, too, and he kept stealing glances at her gorgeous blue eyes in the rear-view mirror.

I should have been more chivalrous and offered to ride in the back with the guys, Charlie thought after a few minutes of being squished together like sardines. But something prideful had swelled up in her after their kiss and even though she knew Luma wasn't interested in Adam, Charlie didn't want to leave her alone with him, either.

With six older siblings, Charlie was used to competing for everything – attention from their parents, the last slice of pie at dinner, her seat in the truck. When she first saw Luma asleep in her bed, it never even crossed Charlie's mind that Luma could want her. Either she'd be straight and go right for one of her brothers, or she'd want nothing to do with any of them. Maybe there was a microscopic chance that she could be gay, but never in a million years would she want Charlie.

Now, that they had kissed, Charlie had a nagging suspicion she wasn't the only one who had butterflies in her stomach every time they got within ten feet of each other. And she wanted to be as close to Luma as possible. So Charlie crammed herself into the front seat beside her.

"I think Mom's going to love you," Charlie said as Adam drove past the apple orchard. "You've got us eating something besides spaghetti and putting our shoes away when we come inside. My brothers are hardly even feral anymore."

Luma laughed and, unlike Adam, who had to look at her through the mirror while he kept his eyes on the path, Charlie had the privilege of seeing the sparkle in her eyes first-hand. She really was breathtaking. Charlie let her eyes linger on the plump curve of Luma's lips and the porcelain paleness of her skin.

They bumped along the dirt road and after about a mile, Luma pointed to the dilapidated remains of a building a hundred feet off the path. "I saw that house on the way back from Grimm Falls last week. Does anyone live there?"

"No way," Adam said. "That cabin isn't fit for humans – I wouldn't be surprised if a family of raccoons took it over... or a bear."

Charlie reached across the back of the seat and punched his arm. "Don't say the B word – Luma already had one close encounter."

She gave Charlie a wry look and said, "I'm not afraid of bears in general – just bears that are chasing me down the road."

"*I'm* afraid of bears in general," Adam said.

"That cabin used to belong to a hunter," Charlie told Luma. "He sold furs in the city. He was friends with our grandpa back in the day."

"What happened to him?" Luma asked.

"Well, he'd be about a hundred years old if he were still alive," Charlie said. "I'm not sure exactly what happened to him – maybe he retired and moved out of the forest."

"Maybe he died in that cabin," Adam said.

"Grim," Luma answered. "Did he have a wife, a family?"

"I don't think so," Charlie said. "Life in the forest can be lonely."

Before Luma came along, that was Charlie's favorite thing about it. The solitude meant she didn't feel the pressure that she felt in college to couple up like everyone else. Being around her brothers and no one else meant she could push her hair behind her ears and get to work instead of constantly worrying about whether she fit in, or whether her appearance was making anyone uncomfortable.

Now, she didn't know how she felt anymore.

"Grandpa found someone, though," Adam said, ever the optimist. "He met a girl when he went into the city to deliver an order and fell in love at first sight."

"Aww, that's sweet," Luma said.

Adam cracked up and added, "Well, she didn't want anything to do with him on first sight, being a dirty mountain man with a long, scraggly beard, but he kept trying. He cleaned himself up the next time he had to go into the city, brought a bouquet of wildflowers from the forest, and tracked her down."

"And then she fell for him?" Luma asked.

"Hell no," Adam said with a chuckle. "She thought he was crazy when he told her he had no plans to move out of the forest and she'd have to come live with him in the cottage if she wanted him."

"It took him almost a year to win her over," Charlie said, reciting the next part of the story. It was a common one in their family and she'd heard it at least two dozen times. The words never changed and it never failed to light a small, persistent fire of hope in her heart. If their grandfather, one of the burliest, ungroomed men this side of the mountains, could win their grandma over, maybe there was hope for Charlie, too.

"And another year to get her to agree to marry him and move to the forest," she added. "They lived in that cottage for forty years until Grandpa got arthritis and his hands hurt too much to work."

"Did they move into Grimm Falls?" Luma asked.

Charlie nodded and Adam finished the story. "They got a little apartment on the outskirts of town, where they could still see the trees from their bedroom window. You can take the man out of the forest, but you can't take the forest out of the man. Grandpa died at the age of ninety-seven and grandma joined him three days later."

"That's sweet, actually," Luma said. "That was true love, wasn't it?"

"I think it would have to be in order to leave all the conveniences and luxuries of the city to come out here," Charlie said. *She could be leaving any day now – don't get attached,* she reminded herself... but it was too late for that.

"I don't know," Luma said, smiling at her. "The forest has its charms."

———

Lunch was at Charlie's mom's favorite restaurant, the Red Hen. They had already reserved a table by the time Adam pulled into the parking lot, and her brothers all piled out of the truck in a rush to get to the food.

Charlie slid out of the bench seat and then held up her hand, helping Luma hop down even though she didn't *really* need the help. They walked a little slower than everyone else, bringing up the rear as Charlie explained, "My mom was never the type to tolerate living in isolation in the cottage. By the time baby number three – that would be Braden – came along, she put down her foot and told my dad she was moving back into town whether he came or not."

"I don't blame her," Luma said with a chuckle.

They went inside the restaurant and Charlie took Luma's hand to guide her to a long table at the back that had become the Jacobs family's customary spot. She stole a glance over her shoulder at Luma just before they got to the table, smiling at her as her chest swelled. *Is this what falling in love feels like?* She wondered, but she didn't really want an answer. It couldn't last, so she was just enjoying it—whatever it was—while she had it.

Every chance she got, she stole those glances at the radiant girl floating through her life. Charlie's heart was begging her to store up as many memories of Luma as she could for when she was gone.

To do what with, she wasn't sure.

As they approached the table, a mouthwatering aroma hit Charlie and she inhaled deeply. Her stomach growled a Pavlovian response as she saw that the table was already spread, family-style, with bowls of mashed potatoes, a couple of meatloaves, and green beans. Joey was already reaching for the mashed potato spoon and their mom swatted his hand away.

"Sorry," Charlie said to Luma on her brothers' behalf. "Things can get pretty savage in the Jacobs family when there's food involved."

Luma laughed and said, "Believe me, I noticed."

"Come on, I'll introduce you," Charlie said, pulling Luma to the table.

Her dad was sitting at one end and her mom was standing at the other end, a large knife poised to cut into one of the meatloaves. All six of her brothers were sitting down, transformed by their mother's glare into polite young men waiting patiently.

"This must be Luma," Charlie's mom said, setting the knife on the edge of the meatloaf plate and coming around the table.

Charlie released Luma's hand while her mom pulled Luma into a hug. Charlie's mom was a hugger but Luma didn't seem to mind, embracing her back and thanking her for the invite.

When she released Luma, Charlie's mom said, "Wow, Charlie told me you were pretty, but you're a knockout, honey."

Luma glanced at Charlie and she immediately turned the same shade of red as the glaze on the meatloaf. Luma smiled and Charlie busied herself by pulling out a chair for her. Someone had saved the one right next to her mom for Luma, and Charlie was sure it was no coincidence that Adam was sitting on the other side of her.

The only other chair still free was all the way at the other end of the table near Charlie's dad. Charlie sat down and so did Luma, then the waitress came by and took their drink orders and Charlie's mom started serving slices of meatloaf in one of the most orderly family meals they'd ever had.

At Charlie's end of the table, her dad grilled Scotty and Thomas on how she was doing in her first month as a lumberjack. He asked question after question, fiercely protective of his only daughter.

"And the equipment, it's not too heavy for you?" he asked as the mashed potato bowl made a circuit around the table. "That can be dangerous, you know, trying to use tools that are too big for you."

"She keeps up with the rest of us," Braden said helpfully from the middle of the table. "I'll admit, I was skeptical at first, but so far there's nothing we do that Charlie isn't learning how to master."

Charlie's dad frowned, probably disappointed that she was flourishing because he wanted an excuse to send her back to college. "What about the work? It can be back-breaking at times. Are you enjoying it?"

"Why don't you ever ask if the rest of us like back-breaking work?" Joey challenged.

"Because you couldn't wait to get into the family business," their dad said. "Charlie had a scholarship she left behind on a whim."

It always came back to college. Three generations of Jacobs men working in the lumber trade was fine – no shame there – but when Charlie got into college, her dad started dreaming bigger for her. He wanted her to get an education and move out of Grimm Falls to *really do something with her life* – whatever that meant. And she might have if the girl who broke her heart wasn't going to be in every one of Charlie's fall semester courses.

Charlie couldn't escape her at college, so she'd

gone to the forest to run away from love, women and everything. She stabbed a piece of meatloaf and said, "I already gave the scholarship up. I'm sure they awarded the money to someone else by now."

Her dad frowned, stymied for a minute, then started in on questions about how boring it must be in the forest for a young woman surrounded by her brothers all the time. Charlie looked at the other end of the table and was relieved to see that Luma wasn't paying any attention to her conversation.

It's been anything but boring lately.

Adam was flirting with Luma again, but Luma wasn't paying him much attention beyond polite replies. Instead, she was talking to Charlie's mom, who was digging pretty deep into Luma's life.

Charlie's mom was a therapist and she had a small practice in Grimm Falls. She had a steady flow of patients and everyone loved her because she had a way of breaking down barriers without making people realize they were being psychoanalyzed. It seemed to be working on Luma, too.

Charlie didn't hear their full conversation – there was far too much going on around the table – but she did hear Luma talking about her family.

"I miss my dad, but I'm starting to realize he's the only thing I miss from Rockledge," she was saying. "Charlie has been so supportive, and so has everyone else. I didn't know that families like this existed outside of TV – everyone really cares about each other and no one stabs anyone in the back or climbs on anyone else to get what they want."

Maxwell, sitting across from her, snorted and said, "If you think that, you ought to be a fly on the wall when we *don't* have company."

"I'm sure you have rivalries like any siblings would," Luma said. "But you guys are *nothing* like my family."

Then she caught Charlie looking at her. Their eyes locked and she smiled like she knew all along that Charlie had been listening to her.

After lunch was over, the Jacobs family—plus Luma—all headed outside and Charlie's dad asked, "Well, should we go across the street for our customary after-lunch ice cream cone?"

Everyone was clamoring for it—it was a hot day and ice cream always hit the spot, but as they looked down the street to cross it, Luma tugged on Charlie's shoulder, holding her back from everyone else.

"Something wrong?" Charlie asked.

"No," Luma said. "The library's that way, right?"

"Yep, about four blocks up," Charlie said. "Why?"

"I think it's time," Luma said. "Do you think your parents would mind if I steal you away from the ice cream parlor?"

"I think the ice cream will mind," Charlie teased as

dread filled her chest. It couldn't be time already— it had only been about a week, and things were just starting to happen between them. Luma gave her a weak smile, but it was obvious she wasn't in the mood to joke. Charlie got serious and said, "I'm sure they won't miss us, but are you sure it's safe so soon?"

"Maybe, maybe not—but I can't wait any longer," Luma said. "I can only imagine the lies Tabitha's been telling my dad. If I tell him not to let Tabitha know we talked, he'll listen. I have to try, Charlie."

Charlie watched Luma's lower lip quiver. The girl was really good at bouncing back and she'd been relatively chipper the last week because she'd kept her mind occupied with other things, but it all seemed to be crashing over her right now.

"Let's go say goodbye to my parents," Charlie suggested. "Then Adam can pick us up at the library on the way back to the cottage."

"Okay," Luma said. They dashed across the street and let Charlie's parents know where they were going. Charlie asked Adam to pick the two of them up and her mom gave each of them another round of hugs.

"Thank you for lunch," Luma said.

"It was nice meeting you, dear," Charlie's mom said. "I look forward to seeing you again."

"Me, too," Luma said, but her smile was a little sad.

Then Charlie led her up the street to the library, anxiety building in her stomach as they walked.

"Antonio said your stepmother would kill you if she found out you were still alive. How can it be safe?"

"Maybe it's not," Luma admitted. "I just have to take a leap of faith because there's a very good possibility she's been telling my dad that I'm dead. I can't live with that."

"I understand," Charlie said, and then Luma slipped her hand into Charlie's.

As they walked down the street, hand in hand, Charlie tried not to read too much into it. This was the first time she'd ever held hands with anyone in a non-platonic way and she had no idea it could be such a powerful gesture. It felt like her entire body was vibrating at Luma's frequency, starting in her palm and radiating out to the rest of her.

Charlie took a deep breath of the crisp afternoon air and decided to enjoy it while she could. One way or another, Luma was going home to her old life, which was a heck of a lot more glamorous than anything she'd find in the forest. She didn't belong in this world any more than Charlie belonged in Luma's. But in the meantime, she was giving Charlie something that she'd given up on.

She was making Charlie love her.

When they got to the library, Charlie stepped ahead of Luma to open the door for her.

The building was Grimm Falls' original one-room school house, converted into the public library after the town began to grow at the end of the 1800s and a proper school building became necessary. It was Charlie's grandfather who had provided the lumber to build the new school, and with the leftover wood, he'd volunteered to build the bookshelves that filled the library to this day. Charlie ran her hand along one time-worn shelf as they walked inside.

"Miss Jacobs," the silver-haired librarian sitting at the reference desk said. "I haven't seen you since you were little. I recognize you, though – all the Jacobs kids have those remarkable eyes."

"It's been a while," Charlie agreed, rubbing the back of her neck and feeling guilty for being an infrequent library patron. "I still have my library card though, Mrs. Marchionne."

"You should use it more often," the librarian scolded with a smile. "Anything I can help you with today?"

"No," Charlie said. "We're just going to use a computer – is that okay?"

"Help yourself," Mrs. Marchionne answered. "Let me know if you need anything."

"Thank you," Luma said. She let Charlie lead the way through the stacks. There were five rows of sturdy oak shelves at the front of the library, plus more around the perimeter. Behind the row of shelves, there was an open space with a colorful rug for storytime, and at the very back of the library, there was a wall lined with computers.

Luma sat down at one of them and Charlie took

the chair beside her. Luma's fingers flew over the keys, typing much faster than Charlie ever managed in school. She logged into her email and then paused.

"He emailed me yesterday," she said, frowning. "It looks like he's been emailing me a lot." She clicked on the most recent email and read for a minute, and her voice was shaky as she summarized the contents for Charlie. "The police found my car where Antonio crashed it. They found my shoes and Tabitha's been trying to prepare my dad for the worst. *Yeah, of course she has.* He says he calls me every day hoping I'll pick up my phone. Shit, I should have reached out to him right away. I can't imagine what he's been going through."

There was a deep sadness in her voice and Charlie desperately wanted to hug her, but it seemed hopelessly inadequate. Instead, she sat still and asked, "What are you going to say?"

Luma answered quietly, careful not to let her voice carry through the stacks, "Is 'Tabitha tried to kill me and if I come home, I'm afraid she'll hurt Antonio next' too melodramatic?"

Charlie gave her a sympathetic look. There was no good answer to a question like that, whether it was sardonic or not. She put her hand tentatively on Luma's knee, squeezing it in an attempt to convey comfort where none could be found. "I think he's going to be worried about you no matter what you say."

Luma nodded, thought for a minute, and then

started typing again, slower this time as she chose her words carefully.

Charlie waited, and when Luma clicked *Send*, she asked, "What did you say?"

"I told him that I'm okay, that I can't come home right now and I can't tell him why. I told him I'm safe and he shouldn't worry about me, or believe anything Tabitha tells him about me, and that he can't let her know he's heard from me," she said. She let out a deep sigh, shaking her head, and added, "Once I figure out if it's safe to go to the police, I'll give him more details."

"When do you think that'll be?" Charlie asked.

"I have no idea," Luma said. "It could be days or weeks. I never thought I'd be in this situation."

"Me neither," Charlie said. "For the record, I think you're handling it really well. I don't know what kind of state I would be in if I was in your shoes."

Luma cracked a weak smile. "I've been in your shoes, literally. I'd be happy to trade."

"I don't think my feet would fit," Charlie said, and Luma's smile became a little more genuine. *My kingdom for a smile...*

10

TABITHA

When Lucca got home from his business trip, there was just as much angst and fretting about the girl as Tabitha expected.

From the moment his plane touched down, he was ready to call in the entire damn cavalry – police, search and rescue, hospitals, everything. The house was swarming with people within a couple of hours of his return and Tabitha had to send Antonio out on the pretense of checking the area hospitals in person because the man was sweating bullets. He'd be a dead giveaway if the police saw him like that.

Fortunately, once Lucca had given the police all the relevant details about Luma that he could, someone connected the dots and dug up a police report that had been filed about a smashed Audi in the forest.

It was a good thing that small police stations in

insignificant towns didn't have the means and police training of a city like Rockledge because they had just towed the car, filed a report labeling it an abandoned vehicle, and stuck it on somebody's desk to deal with later.

Unfortunately for that somebody, Lucca was gearing up to give them hell – the poor bastard would probably lose his job over it by the time Lucca was done. It was nice to see him going all Papa Bear on someone, but Tabitha wished it was on her account and not because of that spoiled girl.

"We should go there," Lucca said as soon as they got word of the accident.

"To the forest?" Tabitha asked, wrinkling her nose.

"What if Luma got disoriented and wandered into the woods?" Lucca asked.

"You should stay here, actually," one of the responding officers said. *Thank you, Officer... Davidson,* Tabitha thought, reading the name on his lapel. "We've already dispatched officers to search the area. They'll notify you the moment we know anything, but in case your daughter comes home on her own, you should be here."

"That makes sense," Lucca said, resigned. He wanted to ride in on a white horse and save the day, but Tabitha was grateful that the police weren't going to let him.

"You have to let the police do their job, sweetheart," she said, wrapping her arm soothingly around him. *Hopefully they do it damn quickly and get this over with.*

A search perimeter was established shortly after they found the girl's car and for a couple of days, a full-blown command center was set up in the dining room. Not everyone got that kind of star treatment when their adult child went missing, but when you were Lucca White, you got dedicated police at your service. Tabitha would never dare wish to be poor, but this was one instance in which it might have been helpful to be a little *less* important.

———

L ucca spent more than a week working closely with the police, pestering them for updates by the hour and sending that brat about a thousand phone calls and emails. If her phone wasn't in Tabitha's vanity, that might have done some good, but as it was, it only made Tabitha want to grind her teeth every time she saw Lucca on that phone.

I know she's your daughter, but what's it going to take to start the mourning process? she thought as Lucca canceled plan after plan to sit at home and wait for the girl to show up.

More than a week after it all started, the police finally started seeing things Tabitha's way. She would have been happier if they just found the damn body already. She had no idea what was taking so long or what was so hard about finding a body in the woods. Did she get eaten by a bear?

It was lunchtime on search and rescue day nine when Officer Davidson came into the kitchen where Tabitha and Lucca had been displaced to the island for their meals like a pair of latchkey kids.

"I'm sorry," Officer Davidson said, his hands on his utility belt. "My chief's telling me that we can't continue to dedicate this degree of manpower to this case. We're still looking for Luma, but she's an adult and aside from the car, there's no evidence that she's injured. She might have walked away from the crash and got a ride wherever she was going."

"Are you serious?" Lucca said, little bits of sandwich flying out of his mouth. "What about the shoes? How far could she walk in the forest without shoes?"

"The case isn't closed," Officer Davidson said, trying to be soothing and failing miserably. "The police force is needed on other cases as well."

"What does that mean?" Lucca demanded, instantly forgetting about the expensive catered meal in front of him.

"We've got to pack up and go back to the station," Officer Davidson said. "I know how worried you are and I'll keep you informed of anything we find out, okay, Mr. White?"

Lucca was unreasonable, demanding and then begging Officer Davidson and his partner to stay. Tabitha, on the other hand, had to try very hard to keep a smile from peeking through her somber facade. The police were losing interest in the case, diverting their attention to other matters around the city, and it was only a matter of time before Tabitha could put the whole thing to bed. Lucca was unsuccessful in keeping the command center set up in the dining room and after an hour of pacing and worrying, Tabitha put him to bed, too.

She took him upstairs and lay him in their expansive bed. She took his shoes off, drew the curtains to darken the room, then stood to leave.

"Where are you going?" he asked pitifully.

She hadn't had a moment's peace for the last nine days. Whether the girl was dead or not, Tabitha still needed her pampering. But she plastered on an understanding smile and said, "You should nap, sweetheart. You must be exhausted."

"I am," Lucca agreed. She thought she was clear, but he reached his hand out, and Tabitha noticed that tears were streaming down his cheeks. "Our little girl is missing. Stay with me."

"I'm wearing silk, sweetheart," she said softly. "It'll wrinkle."

"Let it," Lucca pleaded. "I need you."

Let it?! Clearly, a man could never understand the horror of those words – the amount of damage that could be done to her imported silk dress during one catnap was the *real* tragedy here. But she had to play the part of the comforting wife, so Tabitha sat down in the bed and Lucca snuggled up to her. He closed his eyes and his tears seeped through her silk dress as his breathing slowly regulated against her chest. It didn't take as long as she feared it might, and then she was free to wriggle out and go about her business.

She threw the blanket over him so he wouldn't miss her warmth, and his phone flipped out of the tangle of sheets. He hadn't let it out of his sight since the brat went missing, hoping she'd reach out to him and his nightmare would end. He could do with an afternoon away from it. Tabitha took the damn thing, slipping it into the pocket of her dress, then and went into her dressing room.

Some people would call it a walk-in closet, although it took up a space larger than Antonio's entire living quarters downstairs. Tabitha preferred to think of it as her sanctuary. Her clothes surrounded her like friends and the vanity – her favorite part of the whole house – took pride of place in the center of the room.

She sat down, fixing her hair in the mirror and grinning at herself.

"Still beautiful," she said, nodding her approval. Her lips had gone back to normal and she decided she'd never looked better.

No one suspected her or Antonio. So far, it was gearing up to be a pretty clear case of accidental death... once they found the damn body. The only question was why Luma had gone into the forest in the first place, but as Tabitha had already told Lucca and the police – teenagers were unpredictable and girls would be girls.

She looked at the tear stains on her dress. They very nearly created a relief of Lucca's face – the stain was definitely the same size as his head. Tabitha shimmied out of the dress and said, "Shame."

She draped it over the end of the vanity – perhaps the maid could restore the silk to its original beauty, or perhaps it was garbage now. It didn't matter – now that Luma was out of the picture, Lucca would have no reason to be so stingy with his money. When she was younger, he was always talking about putting money away for her trust fund, making sure she had everything she would need.

The girl had no need for it anymore – that much was for certain. And *Tabitha's trust fund* had a sort of fun ring to it.

Lucca's phone vibrated in the pocket of Tabitha's dress and it slipped down the vanity to the floor. Tabitha rolled her eyes and bent down to pick it up. She retrieved the phone, but when she saw the notification on the screen, she forgot all about the dress on the floor.

It was an email.

From: Luma White.
    Subject: I'm okay – be careful!

Tabitha didn't even have to read the rest of the

message. All she needed to see was the timestamp – it was a new message.

Her fists clenched and she never realized the phrase *seeing red* could be literal, but her vision began to fade as she stared at the screen. It took every ounce of self-control in her body not to scream Antonio's name at the top of her lungs.

What the hell was that brat doing sending emails when she was supposed to be *dead*?

11

LUMA

When they got back to the cottage, Charlie's brothers sat around the living room talking and digesting, and Charlie invited Luma to go with her into the woods to gather more clay for the next week's mugs. As they walked, Luma thought it was a little heartbreaking to meet Charlie's parents and see how sweet they were.

Charlie's mom had embarrassed almost every one of her children by sharing childhood stories about them. She told Luma how Charlie had once been anything but the shy woman she was now, and when she was an infant, they used to worry she was going to grow up to be a nudist because she always ended up trying to disrobe when her mom took her to the playground. She also told Luma about the laughing fits Adam used to have in church, and how Joey had once accidentally-on-purpose belched into a microphone when he was supposed to be singing in the school choir.

Luma couldn't tell if she was trying to talk her children up in a twisted way only a mother would think was charming, or if she was just so proud of her kids that she took every chance she had to gush about them.

"Your parents were really sweet," Luma said.

"Yeah, I'll have to thank my mom for the embarrassing stories next time I see her," Charlie laughed. "If I'm really unlucky, my mom will bring the photo albums with her next week."

"Photo evidence of nudist baby Charlie?" Luma asked.

"Is it possible to actually die of embarrassment?" Charlie asked.

Luma slipped her hand into Charlie's, swinging their arms between them as they walked. The sun penetrated the tall forest trees in shafts of light and during a lull in the conversation, Luma listened to the birds singing above them.

"Hooded Warbler," Luma said, pointing into the trees where they caught a flash of a yellow bird before it took flight.

Charlie smiled. "You're good at that." Then she took Luma's hand and kissed her knuckles. "I'm going to miss you."

Luma opened her mouth—intent on saying that whatever was growing between them didn't have to end when Luma went home. But she couldn't promise that and Charlie set her bucket down on the ground.

"This looks like a good place to dig."

She pulled the small trowel out of the bucket and Luma crouched beside her as Charlie turned over the mossy surface of the forest floor. She dug down a few inches until the soil turned to rich red clay. She started digging it out and putting it in the bucket, and then Luma asked for a turn with the trowel. It was hard work, and the clay was dense and cold. She dug out a couple mugs' worth of clay, then handed the trowel back to Charlie, who did the work much more efficiently.

On their way back to the cottage with a full bucket of clay, Luma said, "I was thinking that you should get back to work tomorrow. I'll be fine on my own and I've been enough of a burden to you already."

"Are you sure it's safe?" Charlie asked. "What if your stepmom-"

"I told my dad not to tell her," Luma said. "Even if he doesn't know why, he'll do that for me. It's only a matter of time before I can go back to Rockledge—you should get back to your life, too."

"What if I don't want my old life back?" Charlie asked.

Luma stopped walking and Charlie scooped her into a kiss. This time, a lot of the self-consciousness from their first kiss had been peeled away and Charlie let herself sink into it. Luma parted her lips and snaked her tongue along Charlie's bottom lip, then gave it a nibble as their bodies met and they both forgot about the clay coating their hands.

Charlie set down the bucket and grabbed Luma's hips, pulling her possessively close. Luma could feel her pulse in her ears, and between her thighs, too. She ran her hands through Charlie's hair, inadvertently brushing her bangs away from her birthmark scar, but Charlie didn't pay any attention to it. She responded hungrily, leaning into Luma as their tongues met and their breathing quickened.

When they finally came out of the kiss, Luma said, "There's one more thing."

"What?" Charlie asked, her brilliant aquamarines telegraphing the desire she was feeling.

"You should sleep in your own bed tonight," Luma said.

"Not this again," Charlie started to say. "I told you-"

Luma bit her lower lip. "I was thinking we could share it." She stared into Charlie's eyes for a few beats of her heart and the thought seemed to be short-circuiting Charlie's brain. Luma decided to play it down. She said with a shrug, "You'll need decent rest if you're going to be chopping down trees all day."

"Umm," Charlie stuttered. "It's a twin."

"I'll make room for you," Luma said.

"I'll think about it," Charlie promised. Then she

picked up her bucket and they walked back to the cottage, a little more spring in both of their steps.

Charlie went to sleep on the couch that night, but when her brothers had fallen asleep, she snuck into her bedroom and slid into the little twin bed.

Luma opened her eyes in the dark, feeling the mattress shift under Charlie's weight as she climbed in beside her. At first, she lay on the edge of the bed with most of her body hanging over the mattress.

"Come here," Luma whispered. "I won't bite."

Charlie scooted a little bit closer to her and Luma opened her arms. She wrapped them around Charlie, pulling her close until there were only a few inches of mattress between them. Charlie took a long time getting comfortable, shifting and adjusting the pillow she'd brought from the couch. Luma waited patiently, and at last, Charlie settled in.

"I've never slept with anyone before," Charlie said. "I mean-"

"I know what you mean," Luma said. She leaned forward in the dark, finding Charlie in the moonlight from the window and kissing her forehead. "It's okay—relax. We'll just sleep."

Only Luma's heart was beating too fast to allow her to sleep, and she could feel the rigidity of Charlie's body as she tried to stay on her side of the bed and keep from overstepping her bounds. Luma ran her hand up and down over Charlie's arm, trying to calm her. It seemed to work—she could feel Charlie's body relaxing a little bit—but the friction and the sensation of Charlie's muscles beneath Luma's hand wasn't doing much to help her pulse return to normal.

She'd been admiring Charlie's body from afar for almost two weeks now. It was firm from a month of manual labor in the forest, her curves subtle, and now that they were mere inches from each other in the dark, she was trying to ignore how badly she wanted to explore them.

Luma closed her eyes, stilled her hand on Charlie's arm, and tried counting sheep.

One... two... three...

Then the mattress shifted and she could feel Charlie's breath hot against her skin for a second before their lips met. Charlie had been the one to close the gap between them, and now that she had, Luma could no longer ignore her desire.

Fortunately, she didn't have to. Charlie's tongue parted Luma's lips, and she put her hand on Luma's back to slide her across the mattress and bring her closer. Their chests met and Luma let out a small murmur of pleasure.

Charlie drew back just enough to whisper, "Shh—my brothers." Luma could see her blue-green eyes glimmering in the dark as she asked, "Do you want to stop?"

"No," Luma whispered back, her hands going to Charlie's head and pulling her close again. They kissed and it was a completely new sensation now that their whole bodies were involved, pressing urgently against each other.

Charlie seemed to lose all her inhibitions in the dark. She kissed Luma unapologetically, not worrying what her bangs were doing or what Luma was thinking. She went from insecure and uncertain in the light of day, to a machine of desire, her mouth, her tongue, and her hands exploring Luma in all the right places.

She put her mouth on Luma's neck and her wet tongue rolling over her flesh made Luma's head tingle. She shivered and sought Charlie, her fingers finding the hem of her t-shirt and inching beneath it.

Charlie's stomach was flat and Luma could feel the faint lines of abdominal muscles as her fingers crept higher. Charlie murmured her pleasure into the curve of Luma's neck, muffling the sound against her skin as Luma's fingertips reached the curve of her breast.

12

CHARLIE

The whole time Charlie lay with Luma, the same thoughts kept running through her mind. *I can't believe this is happening. I can't believe I'm kissing her, touching her, making love to her.* She knew she hadn't fallen asleep, and yet at every moment, she kept waiting to wake up with a jolt and find that she'd been on the couch all along.

That didn't happen, though, and every time Luma slid her tongue into Charlie's mouth, it felt like heaven. Charlie kept the pace slow, wrapping her arms around Luma and holding on in the hopes that she could make the night last forever. She stroked her hand down Luma's silky black hair and along her delicate jawline, pausing every so often to look into Luma's eyes. They were so big and blue, welling with desire, looking lovingly at Charlie.

It filled Charlie's heart with joy and wiped out

every single doubt that had nagged at her throughout her life. Luma wanted her, she liked her, and Charlie was going to savor every moment.

She brought one hand up the curve of Luma's hip and over the slimness of her waist, and because Luma had already had the courage to put her hand over Charlie's breast, she found the bravery to do the same. She let her fingers float over Luma, barely touching her as she glided over her porcelain skin and her delicate collarbones.

She was so small, so delicate, that Charlie felt the need to be tender lest she crushed Luma and realized that it was just a dream after all. But Luma's body was firm against her, her chest rose against Charlie's with every breath, and Charlie watched the swell and fall of her rhythmic breathing. She admired Luma's very existence, her presence beside her in the tiny bed... and the faint outline of her petite nipples beneath the fabric of her t-shirt.

It got cold in the forest at night and Charlie wrapped herself around Luma protectively before she took the plunge. She cupped Luma's small breast in her palm, the fabric of her t-shirt the only thing between the two of them. Luma's plump red lips opened near Charlie's ear and she let out the most intoxicating moan as her nipple hardened against Charlie's palm.

Charlie's body responded immediately. Her thighs became wet and her body was pulsing with desire for Luma.

Then, as if she could read Charlie's mind and knew exactly what she was craving, Luma ran her hand back down Charlie's stomach and her fingers slipped effortlessly beneath the waistband of her pajamas.

"Luma," Charlie whispered into her neck.

"Is this okay?" She asked, her fingers hovering an inch above the waistband of Charlie's underpants. *God, I should have worn something sexier,* she thought, and another thought chased it. *I don't own anything sexier.*

"Yes," Charlie whispered, her lips pressed to Luma's warm skin and her whole body tensed and waiting.

Luma's fingers continued downward, over Charlie's cotton briefs, and they sent a lightning bolt of pleasure through her body as they slid between her thighs. Charlie felt like putty against Luma's fingertips, her whole body surging with new desire with every stroke back and forth between her thighs.

"You're so wet," Luma whispered, feeling it even through the thin fabric.

Charlie tried to answer, but what could she say? All she managed was a grunt—*mmmfh*—and she nearly forgot that her hand was still on Luma's perfect breast. There was something building in her core. It felt like her whole body, the very cells that made up her being were reaching for Luma.

Warmth was budding with every stroke of Luma's fingers, radiating out from Charlie's thighs, and when

Luma took her hand away, there was a physical ache that went with Charlie's longing for her. Fortunately, she didn't stay away long—she slipped her hand beneath Charlie's briefs and then her fingers were gliding through her wetness and the tingling sensation was more intense than ever.

"Oh my God," Charlie moaned, turning her head so she could muffle her words with her pillow. When she turned back to Luma, she was smiling at her, clearly enjoying the effect she was having.

With her free hand, Luma yanked on Charlie's pajama pants and Charlie got the message. She lifted her hips and helped Luma pull them off her, along with her briefs. Then because the only thing that could make this moment any better would be having Luma's naked body pressed against her, Charlie grabbed Luma's t-shirt and pulled it over her head.

She wasn't wearing a bra beneath it and her small breasts with their perfect, pale skin practically glowed in the moonlight from the window. Charlie's heart was pounding in her chest and her body was thrumming with need. She couldn't decide where to look—into Luma's beautiful blue eyes that had so much desire in them, or at her nipples, small and hard, the color of clay.

Luma saved Charlie from the debate, yanking Charlie's shirt over her head. Charlie peeled off her sports bra and flung it aside, and then she was sitting before Luma, stripped bare and completely at her mercy. *Take me. Want me. Love me.*

Luma put her hands over Charlie's breasts, larger than her own. Her palms cupped them, and when they moved, the friction felt like a little live wire that went all the way from her nipples to her clit. Charlie bit her lip, trying to keep herself quiet, and Luma smiled, then shoved Charlie onto her back. She stood up and a small ripple of panic shot through Charlie.

"Where are you going?" She whispered. Was there something Luma saw that she didn't like?

She rustled her hair over her forehead, but Luma was smiling at her. "Nowhere," she said as she shimmied out of her pajamas and underwear.

She had a mole on her stomach, a little above and to the right of her belly button, and Charlie found it charming just like the rest of her – a small imperfection that someone of her means could easily have erased, but which she chose to keep. Maybe she knew it enhanced her beauty – Charlie certainly thought it did.

And below that, a neat tuft of black hair sat atop her pubic bone. Beneath it, Charlie could see a hint of Luma's glistening folds – it was just a peek from that angle, but even from the bed, she could tell Luma was wet and wanting her.

"God, you're beautiful," Charlie whispered.

"So are you," Luma answered, and then she hopped back into the bed. *Thank God.*

Luma lay down beside Charlie, their bodies perfectly aligned. Charlie ran her hands up and down over Luma's arms, her chest, the slight dimples on her stomach, then over the tops of her thighs. Luma put her hand back on Charlie's breast, and every time her thumb stroked Charlie's nipple, her whole body tingled.

Then Luma's hand began moving further down, taking their time over Charlie's stomach and her hip bones. The desire was building up so much Charlie wondered if Luma would even need to touch her before she came. But Luma didn't let her rush things. She tiptoed her fingers down Charlie's thighs, then slid them back up between her legs.

"Oh wow," Charlie blurted as she spread her thighs and Luma found her clit.

"Shh," Luma said, a smile dancing over her lips.

Charlie closed her mouth, and a teeny tiny part of her said *we should stop* because waves of pleasure were washing over her with every stroke of Luma's finger and there were no guarantees Charlie could keep quiet. She could feel everything Luma did to her from her core into the top of her head, and there was no way she was stopping.

Charlie brought her own hand down to Luma's thighs, and she let her knee rest against the wall. She was open and ready for Charlie, and that sight alone sent a shiver through her. Charlie ran her fingers over the ridge of Luma's pubic bone, then down into her wetness. She watched Luma's eyes flutter shut momentarily as she pressed her lips together and tried not to make noise.

Then, just as Charlie found her clit—by accident more than anything—Luma started moving her fingers against Charlie again. Charlie focused all her attention on Luma's body, rolling her finger over the firm little nub of her desire and watching the way Luma reacted to each touch. Her hips lifted, seeking more, and when she arched her back, her breasts pressed against Charlie and activated that live wire that ran down to her thighs.

She focused on Luma in order to keep the building sensation of pleasure in her own body from cresting before she was ready. She wanted to stay in that moment as long as possible, and to come with Luma so they could share every second of it.

Charlie followed Luma's lead, imitating the small, slow circles that Luma traced over her body, and keeping pace with her as Luma got closer and increased the speed. It didn't seem possible, but Luma was even more beautiful when she was naked and vulnerable, completely giving herself over to the pleasure that Charlie was giving her.

That thought sent a ripple through Charlie's body and she realized she was close. Her body was throbbing beneath Luma's touch and each circle of her finger brought her closer to the edge.

"Luma," Charlie whispered. She opened her big

blue eyes and there was the most delicious type of torment in them—the kind that told Charlie she was feeling and experiencing everything just the same way. "I want us to come together. Do you think we can?"

Luma didn't answer—she just nodded and put her free hand between her legs, covering Charlie's hand and showing her what she needed.

Their eyes remained locked on each other as Luma pressed Charlie's palm against her, increasing the pressure. A small moan escaped her lips and she muffled it as best she could then let her head drop back on the pillow as she guided Charlie's finger through her folds.

"Finger me," she whispered, moving the pad of her own finger up and down over Charlie's clit.

Another ripple shot through Charlie at the suggestion, bringing her closer, and she slid one finger inside of Luma. She was hot and wet, and her body contracted around her. Luma had one hand on her own clit and her other on Charlie's, and Charlie focused on pumping her finger inside of Luma. It was a good thing Luma had given her a simple job because she wasn't sure she was capable of anything complex at that moment.

When Luma's body squeezed Charlie's finger again, she let out another small, muffled moan and her hips started to move against Charlie's hand. Charlie slipped a second finger inside of her and when Luma's body began to contract powerfully against her, Charlie couldn't hold on any longer.

Her whole body bloomed with red-hot pleasure and she snapped her eyes shut, riding out the waves while Luma rode her hand and came with her.

Charlie was speechless for at least a minute after her orgasm subsided, unable to move or do anything other than enjoy the aftershocks as her body settled into a profound relaxation. Luma collapsed onto the bed and was grinning at Charlie like a madwoman.

"Good?" Charlie asked bashfully when she'd recovered her faculties.

"Yes," Luma nodded emphatically. "You?"

"Very," Charlie said. She scooped Luma into her arms, holding her tight and smothering her with a thousand kisses. Then she opened her dresser drawer, wincing as it squeaked in the dark, and handed Luma a t-shirt to clean herself up.

While Charlie did the same, Luma asked, "Do you think we were quiet enough?"

"God, I hope so," Charlie said. "Although I've had to listen to Joey and his girlfriend before and I didn't say anything, so they owe me a little discretion."

Luma laughed and Charlie got out of the bed to gather up their pajamas. She handed Luma hers and watched as her perfect breasts disappeared beneath her t-shirt again. Charlie would have liked nothing more than to sleep with her bare body pressed against Luma's, but with six brothers sleeping nearby, she never knew when her privacy would be invaded. As it was, she'd have to answer to the fact that they were sleeping in the same bed.

She wondered briefly if she could get away with telling them it was platonic... but Charlie didn't want that. At that moment, her heart swelled and she wanted the whole world to know that Luma was hers—at least as long as she'd have her.

Charlie climbed back into the bed and Luma put her head in the crook of her arm. Charlie wrapped her in a hug and kissed the top of her head. "Goodnight, Luma."

"Goodnight, Charlie."

13

LUMA

In the morning on Monday, Luma woke up with the sun streaming through the window and Charlie's arm wrapped around her. She rolled over to face her and Charlie's gorgeous aquamarines fluttered open.

"Hey," she said softly. "How did you sleep?"

"Better than I have in a long time," Charlie answered.

"Told you the bed was better than the couch," Luma said and Charlie smirked.

"Maybe so, but it has nothing to do with the bed."

They got up and changed into fresh clothes, then went into the kitchen before anyone else in the cottage was awake. They made breakfast—oatmeal with black-berries from a vine growing near the cottage—and slowly, Charlie's brothers emerged from their bedrooms. None of them said a thing about the night before, so Luma figured they were in the clear.

Once everyone was fed and their lunches packed, Charlie asked Luma one more time if she was okay with staying alone in the cottage.

"I could stay with you," Adam offered when he caught a piece their conversation. "We could rotate."

"Rotate babysitting me?" Luma asked. She didn't like the idea of being so dependent.

"You don't have to think of it like that," Adam said. He ribbed Charlie with his elbow and said with a laugh, "She's the newest one in the business and already she's skipping work. Let me stay here and entertain you while Charlie spends a day cutting down trees."

"Sounds great," Charlie said with a sarcastic roll of her eyes. "How could I resist?"

"Thanks," Luma said, laughing. "But I'll be okay here by myself." She glanced at Maxwell, always the cautious one of the group, and said, "As long as you trust me with your video games."

"Yeah, I guess you're alright," Maxwell said, which felt like a major victory after almost two weeks of grumpy scrutiny.

"Okay," Charlie said reluctantly. "I'll go back to work. The key to the truck is on the hook by the door - if you need anything, you're going to have to go into town and get it yourself, or else run up the footpath to our work site."

"I'll be fine," Luma reassured her.

"We'll be back at dusk," Scotty said as he came over from the table and put his dirty dish in the sink. "Be safe."

"You too," Luma answered.

The rest of the brothers followed Scotty's lead, stacking their dishes in the sink and gathering their lunch bags. Luma watched the seven Jacobs siblings march out the front door, gather their woodcutting tools and disappearing into the forest.

And then she was alone.

Luma had not been alone since... well... when *had* she ever been alone?

There had always been her father, her stepmother, Antonio, the housekeepers and various other people working in the household. And then there was the ever-increasing number of people who seemed eager to befriend Luma. Those people always turned out to have selfish motives, exchanging fake kindness for a little slice of her soul.

If she accepted that modeling contract, that would be another piece gone, and more people surrounding her who only cared about turning her face into a commodity.

But that was a problem from another life – one she had no idea when she would get to return to. Right now, she was standing in the kitchen of a cottage deep in the forest, so far from civilization that even the cell towers didn't reach there. She was wearing a pair of thrift store pajama pants and holding a mug that Charlie had crafted with her own two hands.

She felt grounded, and against all odds, she felt safe.

Luma let out a long sigh, then went to the sink and cleaned up the breakfast dishes. It was perfectly quiet in the cottage and after a couple of minutes of washing, she pushed open the window above the sink. Outside, she could hear the sweet sounds of birds chirping, and the wind rustling through the leaves.

She inhaled the fresh scent of the forest, the pine that was beginning to remind her of Charlie. It was peaceful out there and she could see why the Jacobs family had loved it for three generations.

Luma got dressed and found that there were plenty of things around the cottage to keep her busy. It made a fine headquarters for Jacobs Lumberjacks, but it wasn't really a home. Luma spent the morning washing the grimy living room windows, which looked like they hadn't been touched in years. When she crossed in front of the door to tackle the kitchen window next, she noticed the truck key hanging near the door. She had a second motive for wanting Charlie to go back to work—she wanted to go into town and check to see if her father answered her email, but she didn't want to worry Charlie about it.

As she dragged a chair over to the sink to use as a step stool so she could clean the window, she kept thinking about the truck key. Charlie had said she could use it, and Luma hadn't been able to stick around the library after she emailed her father the day before. Adam had pulled the truck up to the curb and had been honking the horn, much to the librarian's displeasure. But it was close to noon now, and two days had passed since Luma's email. There would almost certainly be a reply from Luma's father waiting for her.

She hurriedly finished the window above the sink and put away her cleaning supplies. She could wash the rest of the windows tomorrow, but she needed to know that her father had received her message. Otherwise, he'd still be worried sick about where she was and she'd be worried sick about whether her message had gotten to him safely.

Luma snatched the key off the hook and took the truck to Grimm Falls. She drove carefully, taking it slow and trying to preserve the old truck's shocks as she bounced over tree roots on the primitive dirt road.

There was no name on it and it looked very similar to the dirt road Antonio had pulled Luma's car onto when she needed to pee. Only this one had a large boulder to mark its entrance, and it was at least two hours away by foot, in an unknowable direction. If the police were searching for her as her father said, would they make their way to the cottage eventually?

When she got into town, Luma parked the truck in front of the library and went straight inside. The librarian sitting at the reference desk was the same woman as the day before – Mrs. Marchionne. She smiled and greeted Luma as if she was a regular already.

"How are you today, honey?" she asked. Her cheeks were big and round and her smile reached her eyes, warm and welcoming.

"I'm pretty good, actually," Luma said, surprised that it was the truth. How could she be good when she'd been exiled from her home under threat of death? It seemed impossible – indecent, even – but somehow, she felt hopeful. Last night hadn't simply been about two people who were attracted to each other on a physical level—Luma was sure there was more to it than that. She asked the librarian, "How are you?"

"Oh, I'm wonderful," Mrs. Marchionne said. "Thank you for asking."

"I'd like to use the computer again – is that okay?" Luma asked.

"Help yourself, honey."

Luma did. She was the only one at the row of computers, and she held her breath as she logged back into her email. Then she let it out in a long, ragged exhale. There was a message from her father.

From: Lucca White.
    Subject: RE: I'm okay – be careful!

Where are you, sweetheart? I'm coming to get you.
    Dad

Luma's heart swelled and she tapped out a rapid reply, losing sight of the consequences thanks to the promise of seeing her father.

I'm in a cottage in the forest about five miles north of Grimm Falls. You have to follow a dirt path to get there – it's marked by a large boulder on the left side of the road. I'm safe so you don't have to worry about me.

Dad, be careful around Tabitha. She's dangerous and I don't know what she's capable of.

I love you.

Luma

She hit send, then sat back and read it over, immediately second-guessing herself. What if her father already told Tabitha about her first email? What lengths would Tabitha go to in order to protect herself?

While she was typing out her reply, Luma decided it was best not to mention what Tabitha had ordered Antonio to do. If Luma made any accusations, Tabitha would have no choice but to retaliate. Maybe once Luma was back at home, the two of them could come up with some sort of truce in which they both pretended none of this ever happened so that everyone could move on.

Maybe it was all just a bad reaction to those lip fillers.

Maybe it would blow over.

If Luma told her father that Tabitha tried to murder her, though, all hell would break loose and Luma wasn't sure anyone would be safe.

"Are you okay, dear?" Mrs. Marchionne asked as Luma headed back through the stacks.

"Fine," Luma said, distracted. "Thank you."

L uma drove back to the cottage, caught between a half dozen different emotions.

On one hand, her father was coming to get her and her old life was within reach. One way or another, she and Tabitha would find a way to put this whole ugly incident behind them and Luma could go on with her life.

On the other hand... she was beginning to like *this* life. The forest really *was* comforting, Luma felt like she fit into the daily life inside the cottage more than she ever had in her own home, and of course, there was Charlie. Every time Luma thought about leaving Charlie to go home, a lump formed in her throat. Did it really have to be one or the other? Or was there a way to blend their lives after all this was over?

Luma drove slowly, caught in her thoughts. And because she was driving slowly, something new caught her eye. About a quarter-mile from the cottage, she glimpsed something red and shiny through the underbrush. Slowing the truck to a crawl, Luma leaned across the bench seat to look out the passenger window at a small apple orchard hidden in the pines.

She stopped the truck, then walked through the underbrush to the tiny orchard. That turned out to be far easier in sneakers and jeans than it would have been in her skirt, and she came to a little clearing where the trees were.

There were only about a dozen of them, but each tree was heavy with mouth-watering, plump red apples. Luma picked one, about the size of a softball. It was a whole other fruit compared to the little grocery store apples she was used to in Rockledge, and she took a big a bite.

It was sweet and warmed by the sun, and Luma closed her eyes to really savor it, not even caring that there was juice running down her chin.

She took another bite, enjoying the crunch as much as the flavor, and then she heard a different kind of crunch as the twigs and leaves on the forest floor gave way beneath footsteps behind her.

Luma whirled around, her arm flailing protectively, and nearly punched Charlie in the jaw.

"Whoa," she said, dodging just in time. "Hell of a right hook you got there."

"Sorry," Luma said.

"Don't be," Charlie said. "I'm glad to see you're ready to defend yourself."

"I never thought I'd have to," Luma said. "I guess it's an instinct. What are you doing back already?"

"I didn't mean to scare you," Charlie apologized. She looked sheepishly at Luma and said, "I was a little distracted this morning and I forgot to light the kiln fire. Plus, I wanted to see how you were doing."

Luma gestured to the truck on the dirt path not far away and said, "I borrowed the truck so I could go into town to check my email. I hope that's okay."

"Yeah," Charlie said. "No problem. So, was there any news from your dad?"

Luma nodded, still not quite sure how she felt about everything. "He said he's coming to get me."

"Oh," Charlie said, her face falling for a moment. She recovered quickly, though, and gave Luma a slightly forced grin. "That's great! Right?"

"Yeah," she said, but she was still feeling conflicted about that message.

Until she actually saw her father, Luma was going to worry about Tabitha. Besides, she was already beginning to miss Charlie even though she was right in front of her.

She took the opportunity to steal a quick kiss, then Charlie asked, "When's your dad coming?"

"I don't know," Luma said. "But I'm sure I'll be out of your hair soon... and your bed."

"You can stay in my bed as long as you want," Charlie said. She locked eyes with Luma and her hand went automatically to rustle her bangs over her birthmark. "So, you found the orchard."

"Yeah," Luma said. "When I saw the apples, I

thought I could make a pie for dessert tonight as a thank you for taking me in. What do you think?"

"I'm thinking that I feel pretty selfish right about now because I don't want you to go," Charlie blurted. Her eyes were fixed on Luma's and she was standing just about two feet away. She looked so honest and vulnerable, Luma had a sudden urge to throw her arms around her and never let go. She did wrap her arms around Charlie's shoulders to kiss her, then Charlie cracked a smile and said, "But as long as there's pie involved, I'm sure my brothers will be happy. Better make two or else there will be a fight."

Charlie went over to the nearest tree and picked a large apple, and Luma stood still, admiring her for a moment. Whether it was from all the tree cutting or if it was her natural form, Charlie's body was lean and muscular, with subtle curves and toned muscles. Luma couldn't tear her eyes off Charlie's biceps as she reached into the tree again and plucked another apple.

When Charlie caught her staring, she asked, "What?"

"This is going to sound crazy, but I don't entirely want to leave, either," she said. She didn't have the luxury of time to dance around whatever had been growing between her and Charlie.

"Who could give up all this?" Charlie asked, gesturing to the forest. She was joking, but Luma agreed with her. It was beautiful out here, and peaceful, and the girl standing in front of her had a way of making her smile even in the darkest times.

"You're amazing," Luma said. Charlie averted her eyes and this time, Luma didn't want to let her deflect the compliment. She joined Charlie under the apple tree and asked, "You don't agree?"

"Stop," Charlie said, picking another apple and handing it to Luma.

Instead of taking the apple, Luma rose onto her toes to hook her arms around Charlie's neck and kiss her again. This time it was joyful. It set Luma's heart pounding in her chest and heat building between her thighs. She felt Charlie pulling backward and thought the kiss was about to end, but instead, Charlie looped her arms around Luma's back and brought her along, landing with her back against one of the tree trunks.

Her hands went to Luma's hair, her fingers gliding through it and sending tingles along her scalp. Luma put her hands on Charlie's hips and let her body press against Charlie's, and just when she thought the pleasure rushing into her head might become too much, she stepped back, biting her lip and looking embarrassed.

When she met Charlie's eyes again, she was grinning. Charlie reached up and plucked another apple from the branch above her. "You want help baking those pies?"

Luma nodded, biting her lip again just because she knew it drove Charlie wild.

14

CHARLIE

Charlie followed Luma back to the truck, both of their arms full of apples. They set them on the bench seat between them and Luma tried to keep them from rolling around as they drove the rest of the way back to the cottage.

It was only around three o'clock and they'd have the house to themselves for the next two hours. Charlie's mind kept going back to the sensation of Luma's body pressed against hers in bed, her hand between Charlie's thighs. She could still feel Luma's lips on hers, her curves pressed against her. She hoped the feeling never faded.

"So, uh, pie?" Luma asked after they carried the apples into the cottage and lined them up on the kitchen island.

That or we could try the whole making love *thing*

again, Charlie thought. What she said was an over-enthusiastic, "Yes, let's make some pie."

Luma stood at the sink, washing each apple as Charlie handed them to her. The window above the sink was open and Charlie glanced around the cottage after a minute, narrowing her eyes. "It feels different in here," she said. "Did you do something?"

Luma laughed. "I washed the windows. Well, some of them."

"They look great," Charlie said, her eyes going to the ones in the living room. "I didn't realize how dim it was in here before."

"It's amazing what a little scrubbing can do," Luma said, teasing her.

Charlie held her hands up. "Hey, I've only been here a month – this place was my brothers' responsibility long before it was mine." Then she handed Luma another apple. "The cottage looks better than I've ever seen it."

"It's the least I could do in exchange for your hospitality," Luma said. She washed the final apple and then turned off the water, and the two of them set up cutting boards at the kitchen island to slice the apples.

"So you're going home," Charlie said as she handed Luma a paring knife. They worked side by side, their forearms nearly brushing each other, and for once, Charlie wasn't preoccupied with the state of her bangs. "What are you going to do about your stepmother?"

"What do you mean?" Luma asked.

"You can't just let her get away with threatening your life," Charlie said.

"Maybe she was just in a foul mood," Luma said, and Charlie's mouth dropped open. "She's got a jealous streak, but she's also a reasonable person. I'm sure once I get back-"

"Reasonable?" Charlie spat. "She tried to kill you. She could try again." Her voice wavered on that last sentence and she stopped cutting apples. "Luma, I don't know if I can let you go home to live with a woman who sent you to your death just because she was jealous of you."

"I can't just give up my old life," Luma said.

Why not? Charlie thought.

Luma stopped chopping apples and turned to face her. "I'm so grateful for everything you've done for me, but my dad's going to come get me, and then things are going to go back to normal—for all of us."

"I don't want normal," Charlie said. "I hate normal." Her heart was tightening in her chest. *Nothing's ever going to be normal again... not for me, anyway.* She turned back to her cutting board. "Slices or cubes?"

"Huh?"

"The apples," she said.

"Oh. I always do slices," Luma said. "Like this."

She demonstrated and Charlie leaned in a little closer to Luma to watch. If they only had a few days –

hell, maybe only a few *hours* if Luma's father was as rich as she said – then Charlie was going to make the most of them.

She squatted down to root through the under-island storage and came back up with a couple of pie pans, setting them down on the counter. She and Luma both reached for the same one and their hands met, and Luma looped her pinky around Charlie's for a second.

"I'm going to miss you," Charlie said.

Luma kissed her, then said, "I'm not leaving forever – I still owe you close to a hundred bucks for my little shopping spree, and I was thinking that one of your vases would look beautiful on my bedside table."

"If you want a vase, I'll give you that for free," Charlie said. She handed Luma one of the pans, then went to the pantry to gather the ingredients to make the pie crust.

The pies turned out beautifully, and Charlie lured Luma back into her bed while they were in the oven.

When her brothers came home that night, the pies lasted approximately two minutes once Luma and Charlie unveiled them at the end of dinner. Charlie tried to make her slice last, savoring each bite, but it was one of the best apple pies she'd ever tasted and it was gone in just a few bites.

She hung close to Luma all evening and it seemed like they were both preoccupied with counting the seconds before they were alone again, and before Luma's dad took her away. Luma kept stealing glances out the window, waiting for her father to appear on the path, and Charlie stole glances at Luma, trying to memorize every curve of her body and the contours of her face. Maybe she'd come back, maybe she'd buy a vase from Charlie and it would sit on her nightstand to remind Luma of their time together...

Or maybe she'd leave and never look back.

Charlie was sorry for Luma but relieved for her own sake when her father failed to materialize that evening, or the next day, or the next.

"Hey," Charlie said one day when she caught Luma sitting in the doorway and looking into the woods. "I'm sure he's coming to get you."

Luma let out a sigh and said, "Yeah. I thought he'd be here by now though – I hope he's okay."

Charlie sat down and wrapped her arms around Luma. "Maybe he's just being cautious. If he knows your stepmother the way you do, then he won't want to-"

"He doesn't," Luma said. "He could never see the bad in anyone, especially her."

She let out a deep breath and Charlie tried not to

watch the rise and fall of her chest from her vantage point slightly above Luma's head.

"I'm sure he's okay," Charlie said. "And until he comes for you, you've got me and those idiots."

She gestured to her brothers inside the cottage, four of them occupying themselves at the dinner table with a raucous game of poker. Maxwell was the only one who had a good poker face – he'd cracked a smile about ten times in his entire life. Poker in the Jacobs house very quickly devolved into a game of who could hurl the most entertaining insult to distract the rest of the group.

Luma snorted as Adam called Scotty a hipster and went all in on a bluff that everyone called.

Charlie slept poorly that night for the first time since she started sharing her bed with Luma.

Usually, she found comfort in having Luma so close, but with every day that passed, and the threat of Luma's father appearing to take her away, Charlie found it a little harder to fall asleep. Her first dream that night was a painful memory.

She was back in Grimm Falls, in her childhood bedroom. She was a freshman in college and she was standing in front of the mirror, adjusting her bangs meticulously over her forehead. In twenty minutes, she was going to pick up the gorgeous redhead from her introductory art class, Ginny.

They were going to their first frat party and Charlie had no interest in it, but she'd been flattered when Ginny asked her to go. They were friends in class, once Charlie got over being too tongue-tied to speak to her, and Ginny had a lot of girlfriend drama during their first semester.

But she was single now, she wanted to go to a party with Charlie, and Charlie's heart started palpitating every time she thought about what could happen that night.

She gave herself one last look in the mirror, straightened the collar of her button-down shirt, and headed out the door. The whole way to Ginny's dorm on campus, Charlie tried not to imagine where the night might take them. Ginny said they were just friends, so they'd go to the party as friends and that would be it. Nobody ever wanted to date Charlie in high school, and so far college was turning out to be more of the same.

But Ginny had given her a flirtatious look when she asked Charlie to the party, and she started using more winky face emojis when she texted Charlie asking for input on the sketches they were working on in class. That had to mean something, right?

By the time she picked Ginny up, Charlie's heart was galloping in her chest. Her red hair was like fire and she wore a tight silver dress with tiny beads all over it that caught the light every time she moved. The fabric clung to her curves in pleasing ways and caught the color of her hair in its facets. Charlie had spent quite a bit of time over the last semester getting acquainted with the sparkle of Ginny's brown eyes, and the little dimple in her chin.

She realized now that she'd met Luma that whatever she'd felt for Ginny was nothing more than a crush based on appearances, but at the time, it felt like everything.

They walked over to the frat house and Ginny put her hand on Charlie's arm to steady her because she was wearing ridiculously high, spiky heels and she wobbled when she walked. They went inside and it was nothing but bodies packed into every room, music blaring almost too loud to hear herself think. The whole house smelled like stale beer and Charlie's sneakers stuck to the floor wherever she walked.

Ginny seemed to be happy there, though. Charlie fought her way into the kitchen and got Ginny a beer, and they had a good time chatting about their art professor, the college, and life. Charlie really thought they were getting somewhere, and when the moment felt right, Charlie shouted over the music, "I like you!"

Ginny's face fell. Her eyes went to Charlie's forehead, a subconscious thing that she recovered quickly from, but Charlie caught it. The music paused between songs and that was the moment Ginny chose to shout her response. "I just want to be friends!"

Then the music swelled again and Ginny shrugged as if it wasn't a big deal. She finished her cup and told Charlie she was going back for a refill, and Charlie just sat there, wondering if anyone would ever be able to see past her scar.

Ginny ran into her ex-girlfriend on her way back from the keg and Charlie left the frat party alone. Back in her childhood bedroom, the rest of the house silent, she decided she would move into the forest, join the family business, and forget about girls.

Charlie's second dream was much nicer, or at least it was at first.

The cottage was empty, Charlie was sitting on the couch, and Luma emerged from the bathroom wearing her robe. She came into the living room, slowly undid the terrycloth belt and let the robe fall to the ground, revealing her perfect body.

She straddled Charlie's lap, put her hands behind Charlie's neck as if she was going to kiss her, and then her face screwed up into a look of disgust. She pushed Charlie's bangs back from her forehead, her upper lip curling—

"Charlie," someone was saying, nudging her arm. "Charlie, wake up."

"Huh?" Charlie muttered, opening her eyes. Luma —the real one—was propped up on one elbow, the sky outside the window still dark. "What's going on?"

"I think you were having a nightmare," Luma said. "You were whimpering.

Charlie circled Luma in her arms, burrowing her face against Luma's chest. "Please don't leave me. I really like you."

"I like you, too," Luma said, returning the embrace. "It's okay. I'm not going anywhere."

Right now.

15

TABITHA

I t would have been a fitting punishment to send Antonio back into the woods by himself to kill the girl – properly this time. Tabitha certainly didn't want the headache of finding and hiring a competent killer with everything else that was going on, but as she watched Antonio sliding behind the wheel of his car to finish the job, she noticed that he was wearing a pair of last season's Armani loafers. And she lost the last shreds of confidence in his abilities.

What kind of moron wears designer shoes into the forest to commit a murder? The kind that was not actually planning on doing her bidding at all – that's who.

Fool me once, shame on Antonio. Fool me twice and I'll have to hire a new bodyguard to mop up the blood of the last one. Tabitha had no choice but to go with him to the brat's little hide-out in the woods and make sure the job got done.

It was tedious, feeding Lucca a cover story about how she had a prestigious modeling job that sprang up out of nowhere, but she needed an excuse for her absence. He didn't understand how Tabitha could go on the trip when Luma was in trouble. The police had been preparing them for the worst outcome, telling them it was very unlikely that Luma would be found alive if she was still in the forest. But of course Lucca didn't understand - he never prioritized Tabitha's career. It was always about his precious daughter. But Tabitha simply told him that it was a professional responsibility and while the timing was unfortunate, it couldn't be moved.

Not for the girl, not for anyone.

Tabitha would have much preferred to be pampered on the set of some exclusive photoshoot instead of slogging through the woods behind her incompetent bodyguard. But sacrifices had to be made, especially after Antonio already screwed this up once.

As soon as they got into the forest, he picked up a rather large and pointless stick and was holding it in front of him like a scared little kid.

"Put that down," Tabitha snapped at him as they marched through the forest. "The police already suspect she was eaten by bears. They'll have questions if they find her beaten to a pulp!"

"It's not for her," Antonio said, his shoulders hunched. "Unless you'd like to come face to face with a bear or a wolf, I think I'll keep the stick."

They were on a narrow beaten path, no more than two tire tracks in the woods, and they'd been following it from the main road for close to an hour. There were no signs of life in this part of the forest, but the girl had given Tabitha a pretty good idea of where she could be found in that ill-advised email to her father.

"It's a stick," she said, rolling her eyes. "That's like a bee sting to a bear. Go ahead and hit one with that and see what happens." *It'll save me some trouble down the line if you get mauled due to your own stupidity,* she thought but did not say.

"So what's the plan?" Antonio asked.

If Tabitha rolled her eyes any harder she'd be playing craps with her eyeballs. "Why are you asking me? I was sending you out here to take care of her – what were *you* going to do when you found her?"

Antonio looked over his shoulder at her, a sheepish look in his eyes. Tabitha scowled.

"Obviously, you had no plan." When he didn't answer, Tabitha hissed, "Idiot."

They walked another five or ten minutes in silence while Tabitha let the steam evaporate from her ears and worked on forgetting how many morons she had in her life. Even in the middle of these primitive woods, they had her surrounded. When she was calm again, she told Antonio how it was going to go.

"We have to find her first," she said. "We'll watch her, see who she's with. It has to look like a natural death so we'll have to bide our time and choose our moment wisely."

Hopefully, they wouldn't have to wait *too* long. Antonio wore a backpack with a sleeping bag and all of Tabitha's favorite snacks – dried fruit, dark chocolate for the antioxidants, and customized protein bars from her dietician to give her energy. If that ran out before they got the girl and she was subjected to anything with the prefix *Mc* from that ant farm of a town they passed through on their way to the forest, she would not be a pleasant companion.

"How are you going do it?" Antonio asked.

Tabitha stared daggers through him. "*I* am not going to do anything." Then she produced a small vial from the pocket of her pants and held it up for him to see the slightly green-tinged liquid. "*You* are going to find a way to poison her."

"Where did you get that?" he asked, his eyes going a little wide. Was it fear Tabitha saw there? She preferred to think of it as respect and obedience.

"Never mind that," she said, putting the vial carefully back into her pocket. "A lady never tells."

They found the house where the brat was staying around four o'clock. They saw her through the windows, completely oblivious as she prepared a meal at the stove. The house was a shabby little cottage, a mix of wood and stone that had seen better days, and it was so deliciously isolated that it took all the willpower

Tabitha had not to run into the house and kill her right then and there.

"I had no idea she could cook," Tabitha quipped to Antonio. "Maybe I'll work it into her eulogy."

It was a good thing she found some restraint, though. No more than ten minutes after Antonio and Tabitha came upon the cottage, they heard whistling in the forest. It echoed through the trees, creepy in its cheerfulness, and for a minute, Tabitha had a hard time triangulating the source. Then she spotted them – seven large men in flannel shirts with axes slung over their shoulders, marching in a single-file line along a worn footpath.

She squinted.

No, make that six men and a tall, muscular woman. Femininity's antithesis.

Tabitha got caught up in studying her, wondering what would make a woman want to eschew her precious feminine wiles like that. Then Antonio grabbed her roughly by the arm and dragged her behind a bush. She narrowed her gaze at him – he seemed to enjoy grabbing her like that, his nails digging into her arm. But there was no time to address that right now. Tabitha turned her attention back to the group of lumberjacks.

They passed very close, only about twenty feet away, and Tabitha stayed frozen in the bush even as she felt a thousand little stabbing pains and realized that her imbecile of a sidekick had dragged her into a pricker bush.

Ignoring the pain, she studied each of the lumberjacks. A few of them were fine specimens of the male species, tall and muscular, and would give Lucca a run for his money. He used to look like them, but he'd become doughy in his old age and no amount of barbed insults could get him back into the gym with the same energy he used to have. Shame.

The girl carried up the rear. Her mousy hair was swept back in a ponytail and that was really her only redeeming quality. There was a patch of red on her forehead, a scar of some sort, and Tabitha thought, *No wonder she exiled herself to the forest. I wouldn't want anyone seeing me with a thing like that.*

All seven of them stopped at a shed and deposited their tools. At least they locked them up at night – if Antonio and Tabitha played this wrong and the lumberjacks came after them, the two of them could get a little lead time while they accessed their weapons.

The lumberjacks went inside the house, the smell of some sort of high-fat meal floating on the air and turning Tabitha's stomach. Then the door closed and she looked at Antonio.

"What now?" he asked.

"Now you dig the prickers out of my ass, you moron," she said. "Help me out of this bush."

He did, the process taking several minutes because she made him stop every time it felt like a pricker was going to tear her clothes. They might have been hiking clothes, but that didn't mean they weren't expensive.

After that, she made him turn around and took a protein bar out of the backpack. While Tabitha ate it, they watched the girl and her new friends through the window. She seemed pretty chummy with them already – especially the girl. That was going to be a liability.

"It's going to be hard to kill her without those men finding her immediately and reporting it to the police," Tabitha grumbled around a bite of protein bar. Antonio was looking at it covetously, practically drooling on his shoes, so she rolled her eyes and told him he could have one – *one*—from the backpack.

"Why can't we let them call the police?" he asked, his mouth stuffed with food.

"Because," Tabitha said, careful not to raise her voice now that they might have an audience. "That would conflict with our story. She crashed her car and wandered into the forest before succumbing to the elements—a natural, accidental death."

"Oh," Antonio said. "Right."

"Start making my bed," Tabitha said. "It looks like we're spending the night out here and I am *not* sleeping on the ground."

The next morning, she woke up feeling worse than after a night of partying in her thirties. There were pine needles stuck to her cheeks from where she'd rolled outside the perimeter of the sleeping bag, and if given the option, she would have rather crawled outside of her skin than worn the same set of clothes two days in a row.

Thank God there were no paparazzi in the forest.

She stood up and brushed herself off, then dug a compact mirror out of the backpack to touch up her makeup as best she could. Sleeping in the forest was no excuse to look trashy. Antonio was sitting on a fallen log, watching the cottage with his chin in his hand. He looked half-asleep and Tabitha wondered if he'd mastered the art of sleeping with his eyes open last night.

"What's going on?" Tabitha snapped to get his attention.

He sat up straight, his eyes going wide and alert as he should be, and he said, "Not much. They're having breakfast."

"Mm, good idea," she said, going over to the backpack. She dug into it, then fixed Antonio with a withering glare. "You ate my dried mango."

"I'm sorry," he said. "I had to do something to keep myself from falling asleep."

"You should have slapped yourself instead," Tabitha said. She pulled out another protein bar and scowled at him as she ate it. She'd never want to eat another one after this.

They watched the cottage for another fifteen minutes or so – just long enough for the desperation to really set in as Tabitha wondered if this was the worst idea she'd ever had. Not that she'd admit it. But then the skies opened up and offered her a golden opportunity.

The front door opened and the seven lumberjacks marched outside, already whistling that stupid song as if they were happy about living in the middle of the woods. They went to the shed and gathered their wood cutting tools, then skipped their happy asses up the footpath.

"Let's go," Tabitha said, starting to emerge from her hiding place behind the pricker bush.

Antonio grabbed her arm again, though. "Wait."

Tabitha wrenched her arm out of Antonio's grasp, then noticed the door opening again. She crouched down and watched as her stepdaughter came outside. Tabitha had to stifle a laugh. She was wearing an ordinary t-shirt, something that looked like it could have come from a thrift store, and even from a distance, Tabitha could tell she was in generic jeans. Sure, she might still be beautiful and even fucking radiant in the early morning sun... but those clothes! *Gag me with a silver spoon.*

They watched the brat close the door, then cross the clearing with a cardboard box under one arm. She looked happy – like she hadn't been exiled from her family and stuck in a dump in the woods. How could she be *happy*?

Tabitha hit Antonio's arm, then nodded to the girl – her best black ops code for *follow her*. They trailed her up the tire-track path for about a quarter mile, being careful not to step on any sticks or get caught in any pricker bushes that might give them away. That was a task easier said than done, but she seemed absorbed in her own world, taking in the sounds and sights of the forest with a degree of wonder that Tabitha badly wanted to mock.

Who does she think she is, freaking Snow White communing with the forest?

When she finally put down her box, she was in a small apple orchard, about a dozen trees arranged in a clearing. Tabitha yanked Antonio behind a large bush – *not* a pricker this time – and as the wretch began gathering apples, Tabitha said, "This is it. Go get me one of those apples – carefully. Don't let her see you."

"Okay," he said. He was still carrying that stupid stick and Tabitha grabbed it away from him.

"You don't need that."

She set it on the ground and Antonio waited until Luma was on the other side of the orchard, then darted over to the box and snatched the first apple he came to. He brought it back to Tabitha and asked, "How are you going to make sure she eats *that one*?"

Tabitha yanked on the bottom of his shirt, pulling

it out of his pants so she could use the fabric to shine the apple. It polished up well, achieving a grocery store shine that none of the other dull orchard apples had.

"I'm going to make it irresistible," she said, holding the apple up and inspecting her handiwork. That would do just fine.

Next, she pulled the little vial of poison out of her pocket and pulled the stopper out of it. She frowned. She really hated frowning – all that potential for wrinkles. It would have been so much easier to poison a cup of coffee or a plate of pancakes.

"What's wrong?" Antonio asked, glancing over at the girl, who was making her way back to the ox with an armful of apples. They didn't have much time.

"I can't touch the poison," Tabitha explained. "But I need to coat the apple."

She looked at Antonio's wrinkled, messy shirt and he said, "No."

"You'll be fine," she said, grabbing him by the shirt.

Would he really be? *Whatever* – he was wearing an undershirt so his chances were probably pretty good. The poison was most toxic when it was ingested, but the odds of him absorbing a small amount of it through his skin before this was all said and done were pretty good. It served him right for fucking this job up the first time Tabitha sent him to do it.

She dumped the entire contents of the vial over the apple, then used Antonio's shirt as a cloth to rub it in.

The apple became even shinier and more appealing as she used the poison like a wax coat.

"There," she said when she was satisfied. "Now go put it back in the box before she leaves."

Antonio carefully took his shirt by the hem, cradling the apple in it like a poisoned apron. He looked worried – such a baby – but he did as Tabitha said, waiting until the coast was clear and then sprinting over to the box and dropping the apple on top of the pile. He came back, holding his shirt out from his body to avoid skin contact, and they crouched down.

The brat came back with a few more apples, setting them into the box, and then she spotted Tabitha's special gift to her. She actually licked her lips, she'd made it that scrumptious-looking. Tabitha could hardly contain her joy as she picked it up – she wasn't even going to wait until she got home to enjoy that juicy treat. This was perfect!

She frowned, inspecting her hand as a small amount of moisture transferred to her palm, and she buffed the apple against her shirt. Tabitha winced, but the poison was powerful stuff. There␣was no way she could wipe it all off. Just a small dose would do it.

She bit.

Chewed.

Chewed.

Chewed.

At first, she smiled. She was enjoying herself. Then she swallowed, took another bite, and her expression changed. Her jaw dropped, her eyes losing that warm, fuzzy expression as she realized something was wrong. Tabitha clutched Antonio's arm, her heart barely beating as she waited.

For just a second, the girl's eyes locked on Tabitha, spotting her in the bushes. Tabitha's heart skipped a beat, but before she could even think about hiding, the girl dropped to the forest floor. The apple rolled a few feet away and came to a stop against the box. She was frozen with her mouth agape, her lips beginning to turn a deep plum shade as the poison worked its way into her system and robbed her of oxygen. She never looked so ugly and Tabitha had never been more pleased to see her.

"We'll wait five minutes just to make sure she's dead," she told Antonio. "Then you'll carry the body back to the car. We'll dump her somewhere close to where you crashed her car." As an afterthought, Tabitha added, "You might need to cut her open and spread her guts around a bit to make it look like a bear got her."

Antonio's face was the same pale green shade as the vial of poison. He looked like he was about to vomit Tabitha's precious dried mango all over the forest floor.

"Oh, for fuck's sake-" she started to say, and then she heard a screech in the forest.

"Luma!"

It was that girl – the terribly unfeminine one from the cottage.

None of her lumberjack friends were around, so what the hell was she doing there? She came tearing up the path and scooped the girl into her arms. She saw the apple and turned her over, clutching her fists under her breastbone. She must have assumed she was choking and she tried to give her the Heimlich maneuver. *Not gonna work.*

She nearly put her mouth on Luma's lips to breathe for her and Tabitha wondered if they were about to have a Romeo and Juliet situation on their hands. If it happened, she and Antonio could carry on with their plans. On the other hand, they'd have two bodies to explain instead of just one. More bodies meant more police and more questions.

But she stopped short of locking lips with Tabitha's dearly departed stepdaughter. Instead, she started sobbing, a sound that was awfully similar to the way Lucca had been crying himself to sleep against Tabitha's expensive silk pajamas. Did this girl actually *love* the spoiled little girl after such a short time? What the hell was it that made people so loyal to her?

"Kill her," Tabitha told Antonio, picking up the stick and pressing it into his hands. When he didn't move, she said it again more vehemently. "*Kill her.*"

"I can't," Antonio said. Tabitha reached for the stick, ready to do it herself, but he yanked it away and then started running up the path away from the orchard.

"Shit," Tabitha cursed.

She left the sobbing girl with the dead brat in her hands and jogged after her cowardly bodyguard. At least the job was done – that was one thing off Tabitha's to-do list and she could deal with Antonio once they got back home.

16

———

LUMA

Luma remembered biting into the apple. It was delicious just like the others she'd eaten from the orchard, a special variety of apple she'd never tasted before she came to the cottage. She wanted to get her fill of them in case she never got to eat them again.

But then there was the bitter aftertaste. That was unlike any of the others, cloying in her throat. Luma didn't remember anything of what happened next. It was just bitterness, and then nothingness.

And then she was sitting bolt upright, her eyes open and frantic as Charlie shoved a metal bucket into Luma's hands and she retched into it. Her abdomen hurt and she had a feeling this wasn't the first time she'd vomited – her stomach was empty and sore, and when she handed the bucket apologetically back to Charlie, she winced with the light from the window.

It wasn't in its normal place above the twin bed—and Luma wasn't in Charlie's bed in the cottage. The window was on an adjacent wall and she was lying on a mattress on the floor.

Her head was pounding and she could feel every pulse of her blood vessels as they throbbed behind her eyes. Charlie set down the bucket and guided Luma's head back down to the pillow as she murmured, "Where am I?"

"The cabin," Charlie said. "You know the one you pointed out when we were going to lunch with my parents?"

"The abandoned one?" Luma asked, her voice weak.

Charlie nodded, then looked around the room. "It's not as bad on the inside as it looks from the road."

I'll take your word for it, Luma thought, unwilling to open her eyes or even speak. Each word felt like a drumbeat pounding in her head. She did need to know one more thing, though. "What time is it?"

"A little after ten," Charlie said, her voice soft and sweet.

"It's still light out," Luma mumbled as Charlie got a wet cloth and lay it across her forehead. That felt nice and Luma relaxed into the pillow. The cabin was quiet and she risked a peek through slitted eyes. They were in a bedroom, bare except for the mattress and the bucket – oh no, that was Charlie's clay-gathering bucket. Luma thought she'd have to make this up to her somehow when it didn't feel like an affront to her eyes to simply look around.

"Ten a.m.," Charlie clarified. It had been around nine-thirty when Luma went to the orchard. How could only half an hour have passed when she felt this bad? Luma was grateful when Charlie read the confusion on her face and explained instead of making her speak again. "It's Tuesday. You were out of it all day yesterday."

Luma turned her head and moaned into the pillow, robbed of any better forms of communication. Then she looked at Charlie again. She looked like an angel. She'd been taking care of Luma in an abandoned cabin for an entire day, her poor clay bucket was disgusting now, and she was still looking at Luma with those protective, admiring eyes. Luma thought she must look like death warmed over, but somehow, there was still a hint of desire in those big aquamarine eyes.

"Drink some water," Charlie said, holding a cup up to Luma's mouth.

She did so hesitantly, nervous about what it would feel like when the water hit her stomach, but it went down easily and she realized how parched she was. Luma drank some more, then managed to ask, "What happened?"

"I came home to tend to the kiln," Charlie said. "I forgot to stoke the fire before I left, and it was a good thing I decided to come back. If I didn't have that

Magic Bean order to fill, I might well have left it until lunch or even the end of the day."

"Mugs saved my life?" Luma asked weakly.

Charlie was beaming at her like she had no doubt in her mind that was the case. "Yeah, they really did."

"I'll have to thank Rhonda, right after I figure out how to thank you," Luma murmured, and then sleep dragged her down again.

The next time she woke up, the light was a little less abrasive and her head wasn't throbbing with such ferocity. Charlie was sitting on the floor at the foot of the mattress, folded over with her head on her hands and napping beside Luma's legs.

Luma reached down and ran her fingers gently through Charlie's hair. It was soft and fine. Her face was peaceful in her sleep, relaxed with an ever so slight smile on her lips. Luma massaged her head and wondered what she was dreaming about.

She let her fingers trail down the line of Charlie's jaw and her eyes fluttered open. Luma let her hand drop down to the sheets and Charlie sat up, wiping the sleep from her eyes. "Are you feeling any better?"

"Yeah," Luma said, pleased to find that she really was. "Quite a bit, actually."

"Good," Charlie said. She lifted the cup from the

floor for her to drink again and this time Luma was not so helpless that she couldn't hold it herself.

"Is it still Tuesday?" She asked.

"Yeah," Charlie said, glancing out the window to read the position of the sun. "I'd say it's around three o'clock. Luma, I don't think you're safe in the forest anymore. I brought you to the cabin because you were too sick to go anywhere else, but your stepmother had to be behind this. She must know where you are."

Luma's heart skipped a beat and the memory of bitterness on her tongue swam back into her head. "What exactly happened?"

"I came back, found you in the orchard. You were already on the ground," Charlie said. "I thought you were dead." She took Luma's hand and squeezed it, and emotion strangled her words. "At first I thought you choked, and then I saw the apple you were eating. It had this thin green film coating it, like poison." Her eyes went wide and she asked, "Do you think that's crazy?"

"No," Luma said as Tabitha's face flashed before her eyes. She had a vague memory of seeing her in the woods, but she couldn't be sure it wasn't a dream conjured from the sickness.

"I had to make you throw up," Charlie said. "I guess I got enough of it out of your system. You've been really sick, but we got lucky, Luma. Why does your stepmother hate you so much?"

"She's always been a jealous woman," Luma said.

"Any time my dad gave more attention to me than her, we all paid for it one way or another. The older I got, the worse it got like she thought I was trying to one-up her– like it was personal. I always just tried to stay out of her way, but I guess this time it wasn't enough. I think she's trapped in this lie and she's getting desperate. She needs me to be dead."

If she could have done it all over again, Luma would have said no to the modeling contract right away. She didn't even *want* the modeling job – but she was being polite and exploring her options. It was what she thought she was supposed to do.

"Oh no, my dad," Luma said, pushing back tears. "Charlie, you don't think he's still coming to get me, do you?"

"I don't know," she said, but her eyes told the truth. *No way.*

"We have to go into town," Luma said, abruptly throwing the covers off her legs and trying to get up from the mattress. "Right now."

"Whoa," Charlie said, putting her hands on Luma's shoulders to keep her from standing. "Take it slow. You've been in bed for thirty-six hours and I haven't been able to get you to keep anything down."

"I need to know if he's okay," Luma said. "If Tabitha's willing to poison me, I can't be sure she isn't going to hurt him, too."

Or hasn't already, a little voice in the back of her head said before Luma told it to shut up.

"I'll help you," Charlie said. "I just don't want you to stand up and pass out."

Her tone was reassuring and it momentarily calmed the frantic beating of Luma's heart. Everything about her was reassuring and Luma was pretty sure there was no way she would have handled this situation so well without her. Hell, if it wasn't for Charlie, she'd be dead at least twice over by now.

"Why don't you get changed into some fresh clothes?" she suggested. "Then we'll go into town and see about contacting your dad. I'll feel better if you're in town anyway."

Charlie took her hands off Luma's shoulders and started to move away from the mattress but Luma grabbed her by the wrist. She pulled Charlie's head down to meet her lips, kissing the center of her forehead.

"Thank you," she said. "For everything."

Charlie scooped Luma into her arms, hugging her tightly as she finally let her emotions go. She was shaking a little against Luma as she said, "I thought I lost you."

"Never," Luma whispered.

Charlie let go of her after a minute and helped her to her feet. She helped Luma get changed into some clothes she'd asked her brothers to bring from the cottage last night. Luma was still weak and it took longer than usual to get dressed, and the whole time she was wondering how a person could feel terror and hope in equal measures at the same time.

It didn't seem possible.

———

L uma changed into a fresh pair of jeans and a t-shirt, used a bucket of fresh water to brush her teeth, and found Charlie in the little living room of the cabin.

"You're right," she said, looking around. "This place isn't nearly as bad as it looks from the road."

It obviously hadn't had a fresh coat of paint in about fifty years, and there was no furniture in it, but the log construction was sound and there was a nice stone hearth in one corner of the living room that had been recently lit.

"Served our purposes over the last couple of days, anyway," Charlie said. "Are you ready to go into town?"

"Yes," Luma said. "Please."

"I have to go borrow the truck from the cottage," Charlie said. "It'll take me about fifteen minutes to walk there and come back."

"I want to come with you," Luma said.

"You're still recovering," Charlie cautioned.

"I'm fine," Luma said.

She didn't feel a hundred percent like herself, and her legs felt a little bit like jelly from two days without food, but no matter how nice the little cabin was, she didn't want to stay there without Charlie. She insisted, so Charlie held her hand out and the two of them walked to the cottage together. The sun was bright and the birds were chirping, and it didn't seem possible that this was the same world in which Luma's stepmother had made multiple attempts on her life.

When they got to the cottage, Charlie said, "I just have to grab the keys, and I want to leave a note for my brothers. They've all been just as worried about you as I was and they'll be happy to hear you're doing well."

Luma followed Charlie into the cottage and stood beside her while Charlie scribbled a note and left it on the dining table. *Luma's feeling much better. We're going into town—borrowed truck.*

She set it under a salt shaker and Luma circled her arms around Charlie's waist, kissing her. "I don't know anyone else who would have taken such good care of me when I was sick as you did."

Charlie kissed her back, then laughed and said, "Well, if it had been up to my brothers, you'd have been eating Twinkies and drinking soda the whole time. Need anything else while we're here?"

Luma shook her head and Charlie took her hand again to lead her out of the cottage. It felt natural and Luma was starting to get used to being there—which was why it was all the more difficult to walk out of the cottage. What if it was the last time? What if she and

Charlie were counting down the minutes of their time together and they didn't even realize it?

She felt so conflicted, her guts twisted in her abdomen—or maybe that was the lingering effects of the poison. She needed to know that her father was okay, and it seemed like returning to her old life was the logical conclusion to all of this.

But she liked the forest, she liked the cottage, she liked the Jacobs brothers... and she was pretty sure she loved Charlie.

Just before they walked out of the door, Luma looked down into one of the boxes Charlie had filled with mugs for her Magic Bean order. Right on top was the silly, dilapidated mug Luma had made with her. It wasn't really fit to drink out of and Luma was sure Charlie wouldn't actually send it with the order— except as a gag—but Luma felt a certain swelling of pride at that non-functional mug.

Charlie had called it a souvenir the night they made it, and for a split second, Luma thought about plucking it out of the box and bringing it with her.

But that would mean she was done here, and she wasn't ready for that.

As they went around to the truck and Charlie helped her climb into it, Luma had two thoughts.

Please let my dad be okay.

And, *please don't let this be the end of us.*

17

CHARLIE

"What do you have in mind?" Charlie asked as they got into town and she steered the old truck up Main Street.

"Let's go to the library," Luma said. "I want to check my email again. My stepmom must have intercepted my last message to my dad—that's the only way she could have found me. But I have to try."

"You're going to message him again?" Charlie asked. "No, Luma!"

"I need to know if he's okay," she said, and Charlie could hear the desperation in her voice. She pulled the truck up to the curb in front of the library and prayed for a solution that would keep Luma from making a mistake by the time they got inside.

Luma jumped out of the truck and Charlie was pleased to see that it looked like she was feeling like her old self again. Nothing had ever scared her more than walking through that orchard and seeing Luma's prone body motionless on the forest floor.

One time when Charlie was young, she was playing daredevil with Joey, challenging each other to do a series of increasingly dangerous and stupid stunts. He jumped off the roof of their parents' garage and broke his leg, and Charlie thought she'd been scared then – at the way he was howling, and the unnatural angle at which his leg was twisted, not to mention what their parents would do when they found out.

But it was nothing compared to the icicle that pierced through her heart when she thought Luma was dead. She was in danger – Charlie had no doubt of that – and as far as she could tell, the only advantage they had was the hope that her stepmom believed the poison had worked and she was dead.

"If you email your dad, your stepmom's going to come straight back here for you," Charlie told Luma as she raced around the front of the truck and caught up with her on the sidewalk. "She's already tried to kill you twice."

"I know," Luma said with a resigned sigh. "I won't email him."

Relief washed over Charlie, cool and soothing. She pulled open the library door for Luma and asked, "So what's the plan, then?"

"I need to go home and confront Tabitha. I'll have the element of surprise if she thinks I'm dead, but I need to know what's going on first. I want to check the news outlets in Rockledge," Luma said. "I've never gone more than a day without talking to my dad. If he's okay and Tabitha hasn't done anything to him—" her words caught in her throat, then she said, "He'll be doing everything in his power to find me."

She stepped into the library and Charlie followed her. Mrs. Marchionne had her silver-streaked hair up in a bun this time and she gave them the same welcoming smile she always had.

"Good afternoon," she said. "Back so soon?"

"We just need to use a computer again," Luma said. "Thank you."

She was remarkably poised despite all the emotions that must have been coursing through her. No wonder a modeling agency was interested in her – in addition to her unarguable beauty, she had the disposition of a finishing school girl.

"Help yourselves," Mrs. Marchionne said. Then she raised a hand and pointed to her wrist. "I just have to let you know that we close at five so you only have about twenty minutes."

Luma and Charlie exchanged bewildered looks. *The days sure pass quickly when one of us is recovering from a near-fatal run-in with a bad apple and the other is sleep-deprived from looking after her.*

"No problem," Charlie told Mrs. Marchionne. "We'll be out of your hair soon."

The limited time they had at the computer was probably for the best – that way Luma wouldn't get tempted to do something stupid like trying to reach out to her dad. She could do what she wanted – leave the forest and Charlie, go home and resume her life as a glamorous model – but Charlie wasn't about to let her get killed before she had the chance to get her life back.

Luma grabbed a seat at one of the computers and Charlie pulled one up beside her. She checked her email and found a flood of messages from her father.

She read through them for a few minutes, frowning deeper with each one, then she told Charlie, "I don't think my dad ever saw the message I sent him. These are all talking about the police searching for me, and... oh God, funeral arrangements. Tabitha told him it's time to 'accept the reality' and they're planning my funeral."

"I'm sorry," Charlie said, putting her hand on Luma's back.

"I have to get home before it happens," Luma said. "I can't put my father through that."

Charlie waited with bated breath to see if Luma was going to change her mind about contacting him, but she just logged out and Charlie exhaled with relief.

"Let's see if there's any news," she said.

She opened a new search window and Charlie expected her to go to a website – the page for a Rockledge newspaper, maybe. If Charlie wanted news about Grimm Falls, she had to go to the Grimm Observer's website. But Luma just typed her own name into the search engine and hit enter.

Charlie opened her mouth to suggest another search strategy, but about two dozen results from a variety of sources popped up. Luma White was Google-famous. Charlie closed her mouth and read over her shoulder.

The first five results were all less than a week old. Charlie scanned through them in chronological order.

Lucca White's daughter missing
> *Search is ongoing for White heir*
> *Wrecked car of real estate heiress found in forest*
> *Funeral arrangements for Luma White begin*

When Charlie finished reading, she looked at Luma. She'd gone even paler than her fair complexion normally was and it scared Charlie. She rubbed her hand over Luma's back and asked, "What are you thinking?"

"That it feels really freaking weird to see people talking about me like I'm dead," she said tearfully. Then anger edged into her tone as she said, "And I can't believe how quick Tabitha moves—it says the funeral is on Wednesday!"

"It says your dad was looking for you, though," Charlie said hopefully. "That means he's okay. Your stepmom wouldn't try to hurt him with all this media coverage watching her every move, would she?"

"I don't think so," Luma said. "Then again, I didn't think she had it in her to try to kill me, so who knows?"

"I'm sure he's okay."

"I just can't imagine what he must be going through right now," Luma said. At that moment, Charlie's heart swelled and she wrapped her arms around Luma. When she let go, Luma asked, "What was that for?"

"You're an amazing person," Charlie said. "Most people in this situation would be feeling bad for themselves, or getting mad at the world, but you're just worried about how your dad is feeling."

"He's all I've got," Luma said. "And you, right?"

Charlie's heart galloped in her chest. "Of course. Anything you need." They kissed, then Charlie asked, "Do you think it's time to go to the police now?"

She kept her voice low so as not to attract the attention of Mrs. Marchionne, and Luma surprised her with her adamant response. "No. I can't risk it."

"The police could keep you and your dad safe-" Charlie started to say, but Luma cut her off.

"You've seen first-hand how crafty my stepmother is," she said. "She'll go to any length to get what she wants. For most of my life, it's been small things, like calling the director of a photoshoot and accusing the other models of stealing things from the set just so she could have a solo shoot. When I was five, my dad planned this beautiful family vacation to the beach but Tabitha wanted it to be a romantic getaway, so she took me for playdates with three separate kids who all had chickenpox just so my dad would have to leave me with a nurse."

"But if you tell the police all of this-" Charlie started again, and was cut off again.

"She probably already won them over," Luma said. "She's got an uncanny ability to see exactly how she can best manipulate people to get her way. I've never seen her fail to wriggle out of trouble, from parking tickets to shoplifting at Tiffany's."

Charlie had a few more objections to make, but she could tell Luma was ready with good reasons of her own. So she sat back and asked the question of the hour. "So, what do we do?"

Before Luma could answer, Mrs. Marchionne came over with an apologetic smile and tapped on her wristwatch. "I'm so sorry, but the library's closing in about five minutes. I'd be happy to let you stay and work a little longer – it's just that I've got a birthday party to go to."

"No, I'm sorry to hold you up," Luma said. "We're going now."

She closed the browser tab and stood up, looking resolute as she walked ahead of Charlie out of the library. They said goodbye to Mrs. Marchionne, who locked the door behind them, then Charlie put her hand in Luma's.

One way or another, Luma was going home to her old life, which was a heck of a lot more prestigious and glamorous than Charlie could imagine, even knowing how drop-dead gorgeous she was and how expensive her clothes had been when Charlie met her. She didn't belong in Charlie's world and she had no illusions that Luma would even think about her after this was over, but Luma was giving her something she thought was impossible.

She was warming Charlie's heart, making Charlie love her.

18

LUMA

"Will you come home with me?" Luma asked as they stood on the sidewalk outside the library. "I don't know if I can do it without you."

"Of course," Charlie said. "When?"

"Right now," Luma said. "I should be there before my father has to go through the trauma of attending my funeral. Do you think you could drive me?"

"I'd be happy to," Charlie said. They took a few steps toward the truck, and then Luma felt her legs go from jelly to full-blown liquid. They gave out beneath her and then Charlie's strong arms were around her, pulling her back to her feet. "Are you okay?"

Luma tested her strength and was able to stand on her own again. "Yes. I think I'm just tired."

"We can't go deal with your stepmother when you're weak like this," Charlie said. "Plus it's getting late for a road trip. Do you want to run the risk of confronting your stepmom in the middle of the night when there are fewer people around to witness it?" Luma hesitated so Charlie suggested, "Why don't we spend the night with my parents, get a good meal and some rest, then go in the morning?"

"The funeral is tomorrow," Luma objected.

"It's in the afternoon," Charlie reasoned. "Rock-ledge is only a three-hour drive. We'll leave in the morning and get there in plenty of time. Come on, you need to get your strength back."

As long as Tabitha thought the threat – *Luma* – had been neutralized, she wouldn't hurt her father. She was getting what she wanted, and if anything, she was probably looking forward to it.

"Okay," Luma agreed. "Do you think your parents will mind?"

"Mind?" Charlie said with a laugh. "My mom will be overjoyed."

Luma laughed weakly and let Charlie guide her over to the truck. "I'm sure you could use a good night's rest after taking care of me for two days."

Charlie snorted and said, "I have six older brothers. I've *never* had a good night's rest."

As she turned the truck key in the ignition, Luma said, "I could take the bus, you know. To save you the trouble."

"I want the trouble," Charlie said without missing a beat. She drove to her parents' house, and it was dark and empty when they arrived. Charlie said, "Oh, shit. I forgot what day it is – my parents lead a bridge tournament at the seniors' center every Tuesday at six."

"Should we go to the cottage instead?" Luma asked.

Charlie shook her head adamantly. "I'm not letting you go anywhere near the cottage until we deal with your stepmother. It's not safe in the forest right now."

She lifted the welcome mat and used a spare key to let them in. The house felt cavernous – even in the short time Luma had been with Charlie and her family, she'd gotten used to so many different lives colliding with each other, and now that they were really alone for the first time, it felt a little like they were the last two people on earth.

"How are you feeling?" Charlie asked. She hovered a little closer and Luma had a hard time thinking about anything besides those blue-green eyes when she was near.

"Okay," she said. "Do I look dreadful?"

"You could never look anything but beautiful," Charlie said, tucking a strand of hair behind Luma's ear. Her eyes lingered on her lips and she took a step closer. Luma could feel the heat from her body. They kissed, then Charlie asked, "Do you want to take a shower?"

Luma laughed. "Do I smell that bad?"

"No, you're perfect," Charlie said, putting her

hands on Luma's hips. "I just thought you might want one."

"That would be pretty nice, actually," Luma said. "I feel like death warmed over."

Charlie led her down a long hallway to the bathroom. It seemed to go on forever. There were eight doors – four on each side – and the names of each of Charlie's brothers on the first six doors.

"My parents added onto the house when Braden was born," she explained, then laughed and said, "and then again when they had Joey. By the time I came around, my dad said if they had any more kids they'd have to start building up because they'd already hit the property line."

Luma laughed and resisted the urge to tell Charlie how many bedrooms were in her father's house, all for just three residents and a few live-in staff members. It seemed like such a waste when the Jacobs family used every inch of space they had.

"And here's my room," Charlie said. She put her hand over the carved wood nameplate and teased, "Pay no attention to the name on the door."

Luma pried her hand away. Charlie put up a struggle, but Luma had a feeling it had nothing to do with her determination to stop Luma from seeing the nameplate, but rather that Charlie was enjoying the feeling of Luma's body colliding with hers, breasts brushing against her arm and hips connecting with hers as they struggled against each other.

Finally, Charlie gave up her resistance and let her hand drop away.

"*Charlotte*," Luma read. "Did you ever go by your full name?"

"Not since I was old enough to voice objection to it," she answered. "I always just felt like a Charlie, and my family pretty much agreed with me. My dad carved that sign before I was born, and before I was even old enough to talk everyone was already calling me Charlie."

"How come your dad never made you a new name-plate?" Luma asked.

"I never wanted him to," Charlie said. "He put a lot of time and care into that one and I appreciated the effort."

Luma smiled, then shook her head.

"What?" Charlie asked.

"You're fascinating," Luma said, pushing her off-course from the bathroom at the end of the hall. "Come on, show me your room."

Charlie turned the knob and pushed the door open, holding out her arm to let Luma go first. She went in, going to the center of the room and turning in a slow circle to take everything in.

There was a twin bed in one corner, a desk on the opposite wall lined with what Luma assumed was Charlie's early pottery, and a small bookcase beside the desk. There were posters hanging on all the walls – mostly bands and a few surprisingly sappy romantic comedy films – and as she went over to the bookshelf to read a few of the spines, she heard the door click gently shut.

Luma turned around to find Charlie standing in front of the door, looking sheepish but with a mistakable look of desire in her eyes.

"So this is your childhood bedroom," Luma said. She glanced at the bed. "Ever bring a girl here?"

"No," Charlie said quickly, embarrassed by the idea.

Luma decided to tease her. "A guy?"

She snorted. "If you can believe it, I wasn't the most confident person in the world before I met you."

"But look at you now," Luma said, closing the gap between them. "Are you sure your parents aren't going to be home until nine?"

"That bridge tournament runs like clockwork," Charlie said, guiding Luma down to the bed and covering her in kisses.

They took turns showering and Charlie gave Luma her high school hoodie to wear because the temperature was beginning to drop. By the time her parents came home from the bridge tournament, they were sitting on the couch and planning Luma's return to Rockledge.

"Well, what a lovely surprise!" Charlie's mom said

as she came through the door and saw them. "To what do we owe this visit?"

"Sorry to drop in," Charlie said as she and Luma stood up to greet them.

"Nonsense," her mom said, pulling Charlie into a bear hug and then doing the same to Luma. "You're welcome any time, you know that. And Luma, too."

Luma smiled and Charlie swelled with pride. Then her dad said, "Hey, you did something different with your hair."

Charlie put her hand up to the side of her head, where she'd tucked her wet bangs behind her ears. "Yeah," she said, smiling at Luma. "It was time for a change."

"Honey, it looks so good," her mom said. "I love being able to see your beautiful face."

"That's what I told her," Luma said, nudging Charlie affectionately with her elbow.

"Ooh, have you two eaten?" Her mom asked, spying an opportunity to feed a captive audience – one of her favorite things.

"No, I'm starving," Luma said. In the excitement of realizing they were alone in the house, she and Charlie had forgotten all about more practical matters like food.

"Well, come on into the kitchen, then," she said, taking both Luma and Charlie by the hand and leading them through the living room like children. Charlie glanced at Luma and chuckled, but Luma didn't mind at all.

"How was bridge?" Charlie asked.

"It was great as always," her dad said, bringing up the rear. "But I don't think Denise and Abby are ever going to end their feud. Can you imagine having a mortal bridge enemy?"

He laughed at the idea and then the three of them sat down at the bar stools on one side of the kitchen island while Charlie's mom went over to the refrigerator. "Turkey sandwiches?"

"Sounds great," Charlie said. Luma agreed, and her mom happily spread out all the fixings on the counter, humming while she worked.

"So, what did you say you came by for?" Charlie's dad asked.

"I'm taking Luma back to Rockledge in the morning," Charlie said. "We were wondering if we could sleep here tonight before we start our drive tomorrow."

They'd agreed on the couch that they weren't going to tell Charlie's parents the details of the trip. It would worry them too much, and it would probably have them running to call the police as soon as Charlie and Luma left the house.

Charlie's mom frowned and asked Luma, "Is everything okay at home, dear?"

"My stepmom and I will patch things up," Luma said, and Charlie was impressed with her ability to say that convincingly. It was almost as if she was used to covering for the woman. Charlie clenched her fist against her thigh, wondering what else her beautiful, sweet Luma had been forced to endure at that woman's hand.

"Oh," Charlie's mom said, sounding wary. "I hope you do. You're always welcome here, dear."

Then she passed around four plates, each one containing a turkey and cheese sandwich piled high with lunchmeat and a generous heap of kettle chips on the side. She got everyone glasses of water, then stood to eat her own sandwich so she could face Charlie and Luma while they talked.

"How long are you staying in Rockledge?" Charlie's dad asked.

Charlie glanced at Luma. That was something they hadn't discussed, but Luma said diplomatically, "I'm really not sure how long we'll be gone, but I'll take good care of your daughter."

When everyone finished their sandwiches, Luma and Charlie volunteered to wash the dishes. While they stood hip-to-hip at the sink, Charlie's mom disappeared down the hall. When she came back, she said, "I made up your bed for you, Charlie, and Luma can sleep in Joey's room."

"Thank you so much for your hospitality," Luma said, and Charlie's mom took the opportunity to give her another big hug. It was as if she knew Luma was holding back the seriousness of her situation.

"It's no problem, dear. Not at all. Dad and I are

going to bed now," she said. She gave Charlie a hug, too, and headed out of the kitchen. Just before she turned the corner to the hallway, she stuck her head back into the room and gave a pointed look at Luma's sweatshirt – *Charlie's* sweatshirt. "Separate bedrooms. I'm not *that* cool of a mom."

Then she disappeared and Charlie put her forehead on Luma's shoulder, mumbling, "Kill me before I die of embarrassment."

Luma just laughed.

They didn't get out of the house the next morning without another meal prepared by Charlie's mom, their plates piled high with a filling breakfast of bacon and eggs. Then she packed them two sandwiches each, a whole, unopened bag of potato chips, and a plate of cookies that she just so happened to have lying around.

"The drive is three hours," Charlie protested as her mom handed over the stuffed grocery bag. "We're barely going to have time to get hungry, let alone eat all this."

"Well, it's always better to be safe than sorry," her mom said. "You can eat it on the return trip."

"Thanks, Mom," Charlie said, giving her a hug. Luma went next, thanking both of Charlie's parents for their help. Then her dad pulled a smartphone out of his pocket and slapped it into Charlie's hand. She asked, "What's this for?"

"Just in case," he said. "I know you don't have much use for a phone in the forest, but if you're going on a road trip I want to know that you'll be able to call a tow truck if you need one. And if you need anything from us, call your mom's number."

Charlie thanked them again and her parents walked them out of the house. To Luma, it felt like they were embarking on an adventure now that they were piled high with supplies, and her heart was beginning to flutter in her chest. Charlie had a way of easing the tension in any situation – she calmed Luma. But the truth was that they were on their way to intercept her funeral and confront her stepmother, who had tried to murder Luma not once, but twice.

She couldn't wrap her head around that fact even though she'd lived through it all.

And even though she'd read the news articles, Luma had no idea what was waiting for them in Rockledge. As Charlie helped her into the passenger seat of the truck, Luma thought she should probably let her go at some point before they got to the house. She wouldn't leave willingly, but Luma could ask her to stop at a gas station and sneak off to deal with Tabitha alone. She didn't want to drag Charlie into this mess and risk her getting hurt – not after all Charlie had done for her.

Charlie set the bag of groceries on the floor at

Luma's feet and closed the passenger door, then jogged around the front of the truck and got in beside Luma. She plopped the phone into a cup holder mounted on the dashboard between them and they waved at her parents, faking smiles as if they really were going on vacation.

"This is weird," Luma said as Charlie pulled into the street.

"Yeah," she agreed. "I don't like lying to them but there's no way they'd let me go if they knew the truth, and there's no way I'm going to let you do this alone."

When they were out of view of Charlie's parents, they dropped their smiles. Luma reached across the bench seat and let her fingers creep up Charlie's thigh. She took Luma's hand, squeezing it, and they settled in for the drive.

"So," Luma said, trying to lighten the mood, "We've got three hours together. What's your favorite... waterfowl?"

Charlie burst out laughing and Luma got to enjoy the view as she lost every last trace of her self-consciousness. It was very similar to the way she looked when they were lying together in her bed, and it turned Luma on a little.

"Of all the favorites," Charlie said. "You started with waterfowl?"

Luma shrugged. "Do you have a favorite or not?"

"The ruddy duck," Charlie answered. "The blue bill is pretty cool, and the name is just fun to say."

"Told you it was a good question," Luma said. "Your turn."

"Hmm," Charlie said, thinking for a minute. Her brows dipped a little bit, determined to come up with a question to rival Luma's. Outside the window, they were passing through the residential area of Grimm Falls and the houses were getting bigger and grander the further away from the center of town they went. Finally, Charlie asked, "What's your favorite noodle shape?"

"*Campanelle* if we're talking about mouthfeel," Luma said without missing a beat. "Or if we're going based on your metric – how fun it is to say – then *pappardelle.*"

She said it in a full Italian accent and Charlie cracked up again. As Luma saw it, she could either turn this into a fun road trip or crack under the pressure of what she was returning home to do. She was grateful to Charlie for going along with her plan.

"My dad took me to Italy for the first time when I was ten and he had business to conduct there," Luma explained. "I ate more fresh pasta that week than any other time in my life and took great pleasure in making all the servers teach me the proper pronunciations."

Charlie arched an eyebrow. "The *first* time you went to Italy? How many times have you been?"

"Four," Luma said. "Twice more with my dad, and one particularly miserable trip with my stepmother because she wanted to be the first in her social circle to own the newest Gucci loafers. Or maybe it was a purse. I just remember her leaving me in the hotel room and telling me not to cause any trouble."

Charlie gave Luma a wry look, then said, "I don't mean to belittle how awful your stepmom is, because clearly, she's a monster, but I can't quite decide whether to feel sorry for you having to deal with her, or throw you a pity party because one of the times you went to Italy wasn't as fun as the others."

"I know," Luma said, covering her face with her hands. "Rich kid problems—that was part of the reason I was considering taking that modeling job. I don't want to be a trust fund kid – I'd rather earn it on my own."

"That's noble," Charlie said. "But take it from someone who splits wood eight hours a day – hard work isn't all it's cracked up to be."

She held out her hand for Luma to look at the calluses that were beginning to form on her palm after a few months in the forest, and Luma kissed her hand. "Your pottery business is picking up though, right? Would you want to do that full-time if you had enough clients?"

"I think so," Charlie said, thoughtful as she drove.

"I'm not messing up the timeline on your Magic Bean order by bringing you with me, am I?" Luma asked. She probably should have thought of that before now, but she was relieved when Charlie said she wasn't.

"Six brothers, remember?" She said. "Something *always* comes up. I built a bunch of padding into my production plan. I'm already ahead of schedule."

"Good," Luma said. Outside, the number of trees lining the road was increasing and the distance between the houses was much greater, too. "Are we outside Grimm Falls now?"

"Almost," Charlie said. "See that house?"

She pointed to a very large estate, three stories high and sprawling across a large lawn. "Yeah."

"That's Grimm House," Charlie said. "The founder of the town built it, along with a lot of the buildings on Main Street. Did you know the town is named after the family that wrote the fairy tales?"

"The Grimm Brothers?" Luma asked.

"The son of one of the brothers was the one who settled this land," Charlie said. "That house is owned by his great-granddaughter and she's the richest person in Grimm Falls." Charlie looked from the house to Luma, and she cracked a small smile as she asked, "So give me a little advance warning. Are you Marigold Grimm rich?"

"How many times has she been to Italy?" Luma teased.

"I don't know," Charlie said. "I sure as hell have never had occasion to talk to her."

They passed Grimm House and it faded into the rearview mirror, and then they were in the forest proper, driving south to Rockledge instead of north to the cottage. The light was a little dimmer there because of the tree cover, and it felt peaceful. Luma had that feeling again – like she and Charlie were the only two people in the world – and she scooted across the bench seat to kiss her.

"I can read you pretty well, do you know that?" Luma said. "I can tell you're thinking that we're from different worlds. Are you afraid when we get to my house, I'm going to go back to my old life and I won't need you anymore?"

"Wow," Charlie said. She pushed Luma playfully away and said, "Get out of my head, woman! How did you do that?"

"I told you, I know you," Luma said. "And you don't have to worry about that."

"How do you know?" Charlie challenged.

"I know because I've never felt this way about anyone else before," Luma said. "We have something special and I don't want it to be over when I get back to Rockledge."

She knew deep down that was true, but it wasn't until the words passed her lips that Luma realized it in a concrete way. There would be no gas station diversions or attempts to run away to keep Charlie safe from her evil stepmother. Luma was still determined to protect her – she'd just have to do it with Charlie by her side.

"I don't, either," Charlie said. There was a vulnerability in her voice and it made Luma want to throw her arms around her in a protective hug.

Luma did the best she could while Charlie kept her hands on the wheel, wrapping her arms around Charlie's waist. "So we're on the same page and we'll figure it out. It's decided."

"It's decided," Charlie said, that pretty smile coming back.

"Favorite salad – egg, tuna, chicken or ham?" Luma fired at her.

"Chicken," Charlie said. "What's your favorite sport that doesn't involve a ball?"

"Ooh, good one," Luma said. She let Charlie out of the restricting embrace and settled into a more relaxed position beside her, their hips touching while she pondered her answer. "Does a shuttlecock count as a ball?"

———

They drove like that for a long time, staying occupied with every ridiculous and minute detail they could think to ask each other. After about an hour and a half, they finally ran out of silly questions and Luma dug into the grocery bag, handing Charlie one of the sandwiches while she nibbled on one of Charlie's mother's chocolate chip cookies.

The phone buzzed in the cup holder and Luma picked it up.

"Your mom wants to know how the trip is going," she said, reading the text message on the screen.

"Tell her that her peanut butter and jelly is second to none," Charlie said.

Luma transcribed Charlie's response, and she was about to put the phone back in the cup holder until curiosity got the best of her. She sat back on the bench seat and googled her name.

Luma White funeral arrangements set for Wednesday

Nothing new there, although it still felt weird to see her own funeral being planned and executed. If she didn't intervene in time, her poor father would be forced to stand in a receiving line while his friends and loved ones—and Tabitha—consoled him.

Luma kept scrolling.

Charity organization formed to honor the late Luma White

She frowned, and Charlie caught it.

"What?"

She clicked on the article and scrolled through the first few paragraphs, then said, "Apparently, my dad and Tabitha are forming a charity in my honor. They just announced it this morning—they're using my trust fund to train search parties and strengthen the city's search and rescue efforts for missing person reports."

"That sounds like a noble cause," Charlie said. "Are you upset that they're going to use your trust fund?"

"No," Luma said, distracted. The word trailed off in her mouth as she kept reading, telling Charlie as she went, "It looks like my dad is really throwing himself into the idea."

"He probably needs something to distract himself from missing you," Charlie suggested. She put her hand delicately on Luma's thigh and she barely felt it because she was so absorbed in the article, trying to sift through it to pull out the important information.

"'Tabitha White is at the heart of the organization,'" Luma read, "'and has put together a star-studded gala scheduled for Friday night in order to introduce the charity to the world.'"

"Do you think she's feeling guilty about what she did to you?" Charlie asked.

"Hell no," Luma hissed. She turned off the phone screen and shoved it back into the cup holder. "She's trying to get at my trust fund. If there was one thing she was more jealous of than my looks, it was the fact that when I turned eighteen, I got full access to my money. My dad's had Tabitha on an allowance ever since I was around twelve and she spent a quarter million dollars on a Bentley just because her friend got a Rolls. She just can't stand being babied like that."

"Are you sure she's after the money? How could she get it if it goes into the charity?" Charlie asked, stroking the top of Luma's thigh and trying to calm her down.

"Clearly, she's resourceful," Luma said. "She'll find a way to launder it into her own pocket, or skim some money off the top of the charity fund."

"Well, the minute you show up there, all of this is off the table, right?" Charlie asked. "So all we have to do is show everyone you're not dead and your money will be safe."

"I'm not worried about my money," Luma said. "My dad is going to be crushed if he finds out what Tabitha's doing. And she didn't even have the patience to wait a whole week after my funeral before she started turning it to her advantage."

"We'll stop her," Charlie said.

"Thank you," Luma said, giving her a kiss on the cheek. They were on a straight stretch of road through the forest and they hadn't passed another car for miles, so Charlie turned her head momentarily and kissed Luma properly.

19

CHARLIE

They arrived at the house around noon, and the moment Charlie saw it, she felt silly for pointing out Grimm House on their way out of Grimm Falls.

Luma was not Marigold Grimm rich. She could have fit two Grimm Houses inside of her father's house. *Estate* seemed like a more appropriate word, really.

"Umm, should I just park on the street?" Charlie asked. Scotty's rusty old truck hardly seemed fit for anything other than the curb, and even there, Charlie wondered how long it would be before one of the neighbors got offended by its presence and called to have it towed.

"Yeah," Luma said. "Park a little way down the road and we'll walk. We need the element of surprise – I have to get to my dad before Tabitha gets to me."

"Besides," Charlie said, nodding at the large, shining chrome gate at the end of the driveway, "I doubt they would buzz me in."

Luma didn't laugh at her joke – she just agreed. "They would definitely have a lot of questions that we don't have time to answer right now. My funeral is supposed to start in two hours – wow, it never gets any less weird saying that."

Charlie reached across the bench seat and put her hand on Luma's shoulder. It was all the comfort she could offer because she was completely out of her element.

"We have to find my dad," Luma said as Charlie pulled the truck up to the curb down the street. She tried to find an inconspicuous space between a couple of white trucks with gardening logos on the doors. With any luck, people would assume Charlie's was part of the landscaping convoy. If not, she might be hitchhiking her way back to Grimm Falls when this was all over.

Charlie got out of the truck first, coming protectively around to Luma's side and meeting her as she jumped out. Charlie looped her arm in Luma's, as much to ground herself in those auspicious surroundings as to keep her safe.

"How do we get inside?" She asked.

"We'll use the servants' entrance around back," Luma said. "I don't have my key so I'll need you to be a distraction for me to sneak in unrecognized. Can you pretend to be a barber? You can say you're here to give my dad a last-minute shave before the funeral. Tabitha won't question that because it's a matter of vanity."

"I can try," Charlie said. She could make no promises because she was having a hard enough time keeping her jaw from dropping as she took in the enormity of the house.

It was even grander the closer they got, rising up four stories and piercing the sky. The grounds were meticulously groomed, with dozens of flower beds filled to the brim with bright blooms everywhere Charlie looked. There wasn't much going on out there, though – there was a shining black Town Car parked on the cobblestone drive at the front of the house, probably waiting to take Luma's dad and stepmother to the funeral, and Charlie could see the silhouette of a driver sitting behind the tinted glass. Otherwise, there was no movement outside the house.

Charlie opened the glove compartment and pulled out a portable tool bag that Scotty liked to keep in the truck just in case. It was small and black, and it was a little bit shabby but it might work if nobody looked too closely. She said to Luma, "If I'm a barber, I need to have some tools of the trade, right?"

"Good thinking," Luma said. She led Charlie along the tall iron fence that circled the property, on a narrower drive made of *commoner's concrete*. It was a hike to get to the servants' entrance – probably about as far as the logging site from the cottage – and with every step, Charlie wondered what a girl like Luma wanted with someone like her.

In the truck, she'd said there was something between them – something special – and she didn't want to end things once her stepmother problems were resolved. But would she really feel that way when she was safe and sound in her own home?

Who could go back to living in a small cottage in the forest after having a place like this? Charlie's grandpa had once charmed a woman into doing just that, but did Charlie have that power?

"You really grew up here?" She asked as they crept up to the servants' entrance.

"I did," Luma confirmed. "See that window up there? Third floor, the one on the end?"

"Yeah."

"That's my bedroom," she said. Then she added with a bitter laugh, "Although now that she thinks I'm dead, I wouldn't be surprised if Tabitha turned it into an extension of her closet."

"I just can't picture it – you living here," Charlie said. It probably had a lot to do with the fact that Luma was in a plain blue t-shirt and a pair of no-name jeans at the moment, sneaking up on her own home. They looked like they belonged together, but as soon as Luma took her rightful place again, Charlie was sure the illusion would shatter.

"Okay, here it is," Luma said with a deep breath as they stopped in front of a large, solid wood door at the back of the house. "Get inside, wait until the coast is clear, then come back and let me in." The concrete driveway ended at a small parking lot and there was an actual loading dock at the back of the house, but by then Charlie had prepared herself to expect just about anything. "Are you ready?"

She asked so sweetly, her big blue eyes looking optimistically up at Charlie. In those eyes, Charlie could have sworn she saw a girl who could do anything, and it made Charlie want to try.

"As I'll ever be," she said. Luma raised her fist to knock, but Charlie blurted, "Wait."

She circled Luma in her arms, pulling her into a kiss. Charlie's tongue glided over her lips and into her mouth, wanting to memorize the taste of her just in case it was their last kiss.

"Okay, I'm ready."

Luma knocked on the door and quickly ducked behind an evergreen bush to the left of the door that was about the same height as she was. Charlie waited on the doorstep, counting the seconds in her head and wondering what was going to come out of her mouth when someone answered. *One, two, three...*

Then the door opened and a tall man in a suit and tie stood before her. "Yes?"

"I'm, uh...," Charlie couldn't blunder her way through this. The man in front of her was narrowing his eyes, sizing her up, and Charlie had only seconds to make a convincing plea as to why she deserved to come inside. She straightened her posture and said, "Mr. White's barber sends his regrets – he had a family emergency and couldn't make it. He sent me in his place."

"And you are?" the man asked. His lip curled a little as he took Charlie in, noticing her jeans and the tool bag she carried casually at her side. It was lucky that she'd given her favorite t-shirt to Luma that morning and chose to put on a collared shirt from her closet instead – otherwise she'd have no credibility at all.

"Charlotte Smith," she said, deciding that she ought to just go for it and do her best to pretend she belonged in this world. She shouldered her way through the door as if she deserved to be there and the man stepped back.

She was in a large and impressive office space, with a nice, solid wood desk in the center of the room and built-in file cabinets and shelves along one wall. There were a few doors branching off from the receiving area and Charlie had no clue where to go next.

"Well, I'd better go to Mr. White right away," she said to the man. "I don't want to keep him waiting."

"Right," the man said. "The funeral's in two hours – don't you think you're cutting it a little close?"

He narrowed his eyes at Charlie again, scrutinizing her. Was he not buying her story? It was a ridiculous one - Charlie knew that. But if he kicked her out right now, she and Luma were dead in the water. Charlie had to sell it.

"Cutting it," she said. "That's clever, sir."

"Mm," he said, frowning at Charlie. "Well, I was right in the middle of helping Madam White with her eulogy. Do you know the way?"

"I'm sure I'll find it," Charlie told him.

"Down the hall, take the staircase and it's the first door on the left," the man said, swiveling on his heel and going to the last door in the row. He opened it to reveal a corridor with expensive-looking wood panel walls. The floors were marble and Charlie could hear voices echoing in the distance – the house was quiet on the outside, but busy with funeral preparations on the inside. The man left the door open, probably assuming Charlie would be right behind him.

As soon as he was gone, Charlie set the tool bag down on a chair and closed the door, then let Luma in. She pulled Charlie into a quick hug. "Good work with Antonio! Did he buy your story?"

"Seems to have," Charlie said. "But we should probably move quickly in case he runs into your dad and finds out he doesn't have a barber appointment after all."

"We'll take the back stairs," Luma said. "I'd bet anything that my dad's in his study."

She led Charlie by the hand over to another door – the first one in the row – and opened it. There was a landing, a turn, and then a wide, solid wood staircase leading to the second floor. Luma squeezed Charlie's hand, then let it go, saying, "Follow me."

"Yes, ma'am," Charlie said.

Luma started up the stairs, walking on the tips of her toes to be as quiet as possible in her sneakers. She whispered backward, "Be careful of that third stair – it creaks."

Charlie lifted her foot, ready to follow Luma, and then something soft and plush covered her mouth. Charlie screamed, but the thickly folded fabric over her mouth muffled it as she got dragged back into the room. Charlie tried to scream again and Antonio spun Charlie around, shoving her up against the wall.

Had he seen Luma on the stairs? Heard her?

Was she in danger?

Those were the only questions running through Charlie's mind as the man kicked the stairwell door shut with his foot. He growled, "Who are you?"

"Mr. White's barber-" she started to say, but Antonio was clearly not buying it anymore.

"You're from the forest," he said. "I thought I recognized you, but I couldn't place you without the flannel and the sobbing."

Sobbing? The only time Charlie had cried lately was the day she found Luma and thought she was dead. Was Antonio the one who'd poisoned the apple?

"What are you doing here?" he asked.

Charlie opened her mouth, but she couldn't say anything until she was sure of what Antonio knew. He detected Charlie's hesitation and cocked his head to the side.

"Is she still alive?" he asked. His eyes went wide. "Did you bring her here?"

"No," Charlie said, making sure not to hesitate this time. If she could sell the barber story, even for a few minutes, then she could tap into the raw emotions she'd felt when she saw Luma lying unresponsive on the forest floor. Tears sprang to her eyes as she spat at him, "She's dead because of you."

Antonio didn't look convinced. A phone started buzzing in his pocket and after a moment of consideration, he let go of Charlie. "Don't you dare move a muscle." He answered the phone, keeping a careful eye on Charlie. His tone changed to one of subservience as he answered the person on the other end of the line. "I know I said I'd be right back. I'm really sorry about the delay- well, no- yes, but- *Tabitha, I'm sorry but we have a situation!*"

He pulled the receiver away from his ear a few inches. Charlie was close enough to hear Luma's step-mother screaming at Antonio through the phone, but not close enough to make out any of her words.

Then he said, "I'll be right there," and hung up the phone. He put it in his pocket and said, to Charlie, "Tell me where she is."

"No," Charlie said.

"It isn't safe for her here," Antonio said.

20

LUMA

Luma heard the door click shut behind her and made it to the top of the landing before she realized it wasn't Charlie who'd closed it. When she turned around, Charlie wasn't there and Luma's heart stopped in her chest. *I knew I should have sent her away from this mess.*

There were thirteen steps between Luma and the door to the reception area. Four of them were old and creaky, and might well give away her position. She desperately wanted to go back for Charlie, but she had no idea what would be waiting for her on the other side of that door. What if it was Tabitha?

What good would it do Luma's father if she and Charlie both got caught within five minutes of arriving?

There were an awful lot of unknowns in the equation right now, but there was one thing Luma knew for sure. Tabitha might make a mistake once. She might even screw up twice. But her pride would not allow her to let Luma slip through her fingers three times. If she found her, she would kill her this time for sure.

So Luma just had to take a leap of faith.

Please be okay, Charlie, she begged silently at the top of the stairwell. *I'll come back for you as soon as I can!*

And then she went on. She left Charlie behind, trusting that she could handle herself and knowing that she might not be able to live with herself if it turned out that Charlie couldn't. But Charlie was so strong – who else could give up a comfortable college life to move into the forest, get calluses on her palms, and learn to swing an ax just as well as her older, much larger brothers?

Luma had to believe she'd find a way out of whatever situation she was in right now.

Please.

She tiptoed across the landing, turning and going up the next flight of stairs to the third floor where her family's living quarters were clustered. Her second prayer was that her father would be where she expected him to be and that Tabitha would be nowhere near him.

She was probably in the 800-square-foot studio that she called a dressing room, pampering herself and making sure she was as beautiful as she could get for all the media cameras that would be waiting at Luma's funeral.

And her father was probably in his study. It was his favorite room in the entire house, where he conducted his business and where he came to think. He'd gone there on the morning of Luma's mother's funeral.

Luma was a newborn, only seven days old, so of course, she had no memory of it, but her father had hired a photographer to take tasteful photographs of the day because he thought it would help them both to grieve her better.

Luma had no idea if it had helped or not – she was five the first time her father showed her the photo album from that day. The important part was the fact that almost every photograph from before they'd left to go to the funeral home had her father's study as its background. That was why Luma was sure he'd be there now.

She opened the door to the third-floor hallway slowly, just a few inches at first. Luma's bedroom was the first door on the right. On the left, there was her old playroom, which she'd outgrown around the age of twelve and hadn't visited in years, and then her personal library where she'd spent quite a lot of time.

Everything was quiet there, so she inched the door open a little further and stepped into the hallway, closing it silently behind her. She took a deep breath, hearing her pulse in her ears. At the opposite end of the hall, there was the master suite – a large bedroom, a massive closet that could well have been a room of its own, plus Luma's father's bathroom and a separate, enormous dressing room for Tabitha containing everything one could expect in a professional salon.

And just across the hall, there was Luma's father's study.

She'd never been so afraid as she tiptoed down the hallway in her own house – even more than being left in the woods and told to disappear under threat of death. Charlie was never far from Luma's mind, but she tried not to wonder what was happening to her. It wasn't constructive and it wouldn't do either of them any good if Luma got distracted and didn't reach her father. Then whatever Charlie was being put through would be for nothing.

As Luma got closer to her father's study, she heard the sound of water running in Tabitha's dressing room. Luma imagined her sitting at her vanity just feet away. Would the hair on the back of her neck stand up when Luma got near? Could Tabitha sense her?

No, Luma told herself. *That's ridiculous. She's heartless, but she doesn't have superpowers.*

She kept walking. Her legs felt like they'd turned to wood and her knees didn't want to bend.

Keep going, she told herself. *Just a little farther.*

"*Now* who's the fairest in this house?" she could hear Tabitha say, her voice muffled through the door. There was steam coming into the hallway in thin tendrils beneath the door and the hall smelled like a thousand different cosmetic products. It was a cloying smell, overwhelming, and Luma moved a little faster past the door.

"You've always been the most beautiful one of my clients," someone else, a female voice, said in a patronizing tone. "Anyone can see you're a queen."

"Damn straight," Tabitha agreed. Then she snapped, "Fix this loose hair. I will not be photographed with fly-aways!"

"Yes, madam," the woman said. Luma didn't know all of the people on Tabitha's beauty team – there were so many people whose whole lives were dedicated to her appearance – but every one of them was a committed suck-up. Tabitha would have it no other way.

At least she's occupied with her hair, Luma thought as she reached for the handle of the study door. She closed her eyes, said a quick prayer, then opened it. The door squeaked on its old hinges and she winced at the sound, but it would all be over in a moment. Her dad would look up from his desk, his eyes would flood with relieved tears, and he'd come running to Luma. Once he saw that she was alive, Tabitha couldn't touch her.

"Dad?" She asked as she stepped into the study. "Dad?"

But the room was empty and dark. Her heart started pounding again as she looked frantically around the room. He wasn't at his desk, he wasn't in the plush leather chair where he liked to read, and the conference table where he conducted business was bare. He wasn't there.

He wasn't-

Luma felt cold, bony hands closing around her neck, fingernails shaped like talons digging into her flesh.

21

TABITHA

When Tabitha heard the brat's voice in the hallway, her blood ran cold.

Dad? Dad? Ugh, kill me... or more like, kill her, and then kill Antonio because that man is completely useless!

How could she *still* not be dead? She was like a cockroach. Tabitha flew out of her chair so fast she left her stylist holding a comb in mid-air.

"Don't move a muscle!" Tabitha snapped at her stylist. "I'll be right back."

She could tell something was wrong when she talked to Antonio on the phone a minute ago. Did he know about this? She went into the hallway. She knew exactly what she would find when she got there, and yet she still had a hard time believing her eyes. Her supposed-to-be-dead stepdaughter was standing with her back to Tabitha just inside the study, expecting to see her father.

Good thing Lucca already left to make sure everything at the funeral home was coming together as he wanted. Tabitha told him at the time he was worrying too much—it annoyed her that he cared so much about such unimportant details as to whether his daughter's favorite flowers were at the altar, or whether the empty urn they were using was shined up properly. Now, though, Tabitha was glad he was gone.

It gave her free reign to do what she had to in order to get rid of this nuisance once and for all. Tabitha took great pleasure in closing her fingers around the girl's neck. It was so small and dainty that she had no trouble bringing her fingers together over her windpipe.

She squeezed. As hard as she could.

A strangled gasp came from her compressed throat and Tabitha shoved her further into the room so she could kick the door shut. The last thing she needed was for her stylist to hear all this and disobey her order to stay put.

She shoved Luma over to the wall, where there was a fireplace with a mirror above the mantel. She was facing away from Tabitha, but she wanted to see the look in the wretch's eyes when she realized there was no way to wriggle out of the situation this time. She was going to die.

Her eyes were wild, casting about for anything she

could use to defend herself, no doubt. Tabitha snapped, "Look at me!"

She did. Her body stilled but her hands kept flailing. She was clawing at Tabitha, trying to pry her fingers away from her windpipe. She was getting frantic, desperate to draw her next breath. Her lips were turning a horrific shade of purple.

"You look like shit," Tabitha said with a small laugh. "That makes me very happy."

The girl noticed Tabitha's distraction and chose that moment to swing one leg backward, the heel of her sneaker narrowly avoiding Tabitha's shin. She squeezed a little tighter and made her keep looking at herself in the mirror. *Watch yourself die, brat.*

Tabitha looked pretty good, even with half-styled hair. Black really was her color, and the designer cocktail dress she'd chosen for the funeral accentuated all of her angles in a way only the finest fabrics could.

A sharp pain tore across her middle finger, snapping Tabitha out of her own reflection.

"Ouch!" She hissed, throwing the girl to the hard marble hearth and looking at her hand.

The little bitch scratched her, and that would not do at all. Tabitha couldn't very well show up to her stepdaughter's funeral looking like she'd gotten into an altercation with a badger on her way there. She put her finger to her mouth, sucking the blood from the scratch while she watched the girl gasp for air with her hands at her throat.

She couldn't let her regain her bearings, even though it would be fun to toy with her a little bit. Her stylist was too near and she might hear any cries for help the wretch managed to croak out.

The next time she looked up at Tabitha, horror and pleading in her eyes, Tabitha backhanded her, feeling the large diamonds in her engagement ring snag their way through her flesh. *Well, that was satisfying.*

The girl turned her head away, one hand on her cheek, and Tabitha took off the chunky chain necklace she was wearing. It was a statement piece, and it really was the perfect complement to her dress. It was also thick and strong, and it would do the job that a poison apple couldn't. As Tabitha twirled it around her fists, she wondered if she would have the audacity to put it back on her neck and wear it to the funeral after she was through with the girl.

I just might.

She looped the chain around her neck, knocking her hand out of the way, and then before she had a chance to yell, Tabitha twisted it hard behind her neck. She struggled at first, her legs kicking and losing their grip on the marble. She tried to get her hands around the chain – Tabitha wasn't about to let the wretch scratch her twice – but it was too late and she was too desperate.

It didn't take long for her to go limp, her lips nearing cerulean blue. Of course, it would be just like her to be beautiful in death. Tabitha took the necklace back, pleased to see that it had left a deep purple groove in her neck but the chain itself was entirely unscathed. She lay it on the mantel, then took the girl by the wrists and dragged her to a closet a few feet away. Thankfully it was only a few feet – dead weight was harder to move than the movies made it seem.

Tabitha shoved her into the closet, just a tangle of limbs for Antonio to deal with while she joined her poor, grieving husband at the funeral. At least now it would be an honest event.

Pushing the closet door shut, Tabitha smoothed her dress and frowned at the scratch on her finger. There was nothing she could do about that, but it was a small price to pay for *finally* getting the job done. *If you want something done right, you have to do it yourself* – clearly, that old maxim was still true.

She decided the scratch wouldn't be that hard to explain after all. She'd cut her finger on one of the Swarovski crystals sewn into the collar of her dress while her stylist was helping her into it. Simple and believable.

Tabitha went over to the mirror and picked up the necklace. She checked it again for blood – or anything that could tie her to this moment – but it was impeccable. She hung it back on her neck, taking care to adjust it properly in the mirror. Then she smiled, primped her hair and walked back across the hall to finish getting ready for the funeral.

22

CHARLIE

Antonio had to fight Charlie into the chair. He inadvertently knocked her over in the process and sent her careening into the arm of the wooden chair. It smashed into her spine and sent pain down into her tailbone, but Antonio didn't waver.

"Please don't do this," Charlie had said as he tied her hands behind her back. He'd improvised, using his own necktie while Charlie protested, "Let me go and we can work together to keep her safe."

Antonio was afraid of Tabitha, but he cared about Luma. Charlie had seen it in his eyes, but it didn't override his fear of Tabitha. He was willing to do whatever she told him to and that included tying Charlie up and sticking her in a closet to be dealt with later.

"I'm sorry, it has to be this way," Antonio said just before he shut the door.

Then the little coat closet was pitched into darkness and Charlie was alone. Her back was aching and she heard the soles of Antonio's loafers clack across the floor. A door creaked open and his phone started buzzing again. He paused, and Charlie picked up snippets of his side of the conversation.

They included the bone-chilling questions, "In the study?" and, "You're sure she's dead?"

On the other end of the line, Tabitha screeched so loudly that Charlie heard, clear as day, the words, *"Do it right this time!"*

Charlie could barely breathe as she summoned all of her strength and ripped her hands free from the restraints. The friction burned her wrists but she didn't even pause as she kicked the door open. The wood splintered in the frame and Charlie was lucky the reception room was empty. Antonio had already gone on his way and Charlie had only one mission - get to the study before he did.

Please be okay, Luma. Please!

The house seemed to have gone quiet. Charlie didn't hear the echo of voices down the hall anymore, and it seemed like a safe bet that, if she took the time to go around the front of the house and look in the driveway, the Town Car would be gone. Tabitha and Luma's father had gone to the funeral.

Not that she had time for any of that.

Her only hope was that she could sprint up the

back staircase faster than Tabitha's lackey could get to the study from the other direction. Charlie took the stairs three at a time, ignoring the burning in her thighs as she raced up to the third floor. That was all she knew, and she was at a distinct disadvantage because Antonio knew the layout of the house.

When Charlie got to the third floor, everything was quiet there, too.

A few of the doors were open and that helped. She peeked her head in and when she saw they were empty, she moved on. Charlie hissed Luma's name as she went, calling for her as loud as she dared and praying for a response. *She can't be dead. Luma, you can't be dead!*

She was expecting to come face-to-face with Antonio at any moment, and this was exactly why Charlie had lied to her parents about what she was coming to Rockledge to do – her mother would be in full panic mode right now if she knew what was happening. All Charlie could do was channel the stoicism of her most level-headed brother. *Be serious like Braden, and maybe a little mean like Maxwell.*

The hallway was long with a staircase at the other end. Where was Antonio and how much of a lead did Charlie have?

She refused to think about the alternative – that he had the lead and she was bumbling through an empty corridor after he'd already snatched Luma away. At the end of the hall, there was one more door, and Antonio was just coming up the stairs.

"Hey!" he barked when he spotted Charlie. "How did you get up here?"

Charlie's heart was pounding and there was not a thought in her mind except for Luma's safety. There was a small, decorative table pushed up against the wall beside her, a couple of silver candlesticks on it holding candles that had never been lit. Charlie pulled both the candles out and chucked them one after the other at Antonio to slow him down. He dodged the first one and got hit by the second.

"Stop!" Antonio shouted, holding his hands up defensively. "I don't want to hurt you."

Any more, Charlie thought. She ignored him and raised her voice as she called, "Luma! Where are you?"

There was no answer and Antonio was on the landing now. Charlie dodged into the last door at the end of the hall. The room was dark but she could make out walls lined with bookshelves, and a large desk as the focal point in front of a row of tall windows. This had to be the study, but where was-

"Luma!"

The word barely came out of Charlie's mouth. It was more like a scream abandoned halfway through as she spotted a porcelain-skinned arm on the floor, peeking out of a half-opened closet door. Charlie thought her legs would melt long before she got to

Luma, but somehow she managed. She threw open the door and scooped Luma into her arms.

Not again, not again, not again...

She was limp against Charlie and her beautiful, plump lips had gone blue. She wasn't breathing, there was no pulse in her throat, and this time, there were deep, vicious purple marks on her neck.

"No, Luma, you can't leave me," Charlie mumbled as tears streamed down her cheeks and bled into her shirt. Her heart was turning into a hard little lump of charcoal in her chest as she realized what was happening – she was too late.

I never even got the chance to tell you I love you.

Charlie looked over her shoulder, expecting Antonio to be rushing at her with one of the candlesticks raised as a weapon. Instead, he was walking slowly into the room, horror written all over his face. "Is she...?"

"No," Charlie said, shaking her head violently as she cradled Luma. "No, she can't be! Call 911."

Instead, Antonio dropped to his knees just inside the door. "Oh, God. What have I done?"

"Call an ambulance!" Charlie shouted at him, but he was lost in his own misery.

"I never should have left her in the forest," he said. "I should have stood up to Tabitha."

Charlie realized he wasn't going to be any help, and though her lips may be blue and her body was still, Charlie wasn't done fighting for Luma. A strange, efficient calm descended over her as she realized she knew exactly what to do. Charlie lay Luma on her back, tilting her head for maximum airflow, and pulled her dad's phone out of her pocket – thank God for overprotective parents.

She dialed 911 and put the phone on the floor with the speakerphone on, doing her best to rein in the overwhelming emotions coursing through her as she told the operator everything they needed to know.

"I'm at the White estate. Luma White has been strangled. She's not breathing – I need an ambulance, and I need you to talk me through CPR until the paramedics get here."

The words didn't sound like they were coming from Charlie's mouth. She easily could have pictured Braden dispassionately relaying that information, but Charlie? Antonio had crumpled into a rocking, neurotic puddle on the floor and Charlie ignored him, trying to save Luma.

"Please fight, Luma," she told her as she used her fingers the way the emergency operator told her to find the proper place to start chest compressions. "You can't let that horrible woman win. Come back to me."

While she carefully counted compressions and waited for the ambulance, Charlie noticed Antonio talking behind her. Blubbering, was more like it. He was on his phone after all, not with the emergency responders but with Luma's father, from what it sounded like.

"Please forgive me," he was crying. "I was just trying to protect her. I didn't mean for any of this to happen."

The paramedics came fast – a lot faster than they would have shown up if Charlie and Luma had been in the woods when this happened. Charlie was just starting to send up a prayer of thanks for that small miracle when one of them shook his head and said, "I'm sorry, she's gone."

"What?" Charlie asked. She was still doing the compressions and breathing that the operator had taught her, waiting for one of them to take over. But he just stood up, looking at her sadly, and gestured for the other two paramedics to come forward with the stretcher. There was no urgency in their movements. "No! You have to save her!"

"She's got no pulse," he said. "Even if we could bring her back, it's been too long. The likelihood that she'd be braindead-"

"You're going to bring her back!" Charlie shouted at him. She grabbed his wrist and yanked him back down to the floor, putting his palm on Luma's chest where her own had been. "Do the chest compressions! Breathe for her! *Do everything you can – this is Lucca White's daughter, for fuck sake, and she can't die!"*

Charlie didn't care about Luma's family connections, but they seemed to mean something to the paramedic. He nodded at her, then started compressions.

"Hey, get over here and intubate," he barked to one

of the others, then to the third, he said, "Bring that stretcher!"

Relieved, Charlie moved out of the way, going over to the door where Antonio was sitting with his back up against the wall, looking like he'd given up on life. Charlie's legs were feeling like jelly again but she ignored them – all that mattered was Luma. It was hard to watch the paramedics insert the long metal hook into her throat to intubate her. Charlie nearly gagged when the paramedic pulled it back out, but Luma remained motionless.

He hooked a rubber bulb to the tube he'd placed in her throat and began squeezing it at regular intervals, breathing for her. Without even realizing she was doing it, Charlie's own breathing synced with each squeeze of oxygen the paramedic gave to Luma.

Please breathe, Charlie thought. *Please just breathe, baby.*

Luma's father arrived just as the paramedics were carrying the stretcher down the long staircase. He rushed to Luma's side, but one of the paramedics ushered him away from the stretcher, saying, "Sir, please—we're trying to save your daughter but time is of the essence. You can meet us at the hospital, okay?"

"Luma," he said, reaching for her as he watched them continue carrying her down the stairs. Charlie was bringing up the rear behind the stretcher, hardly breathing herself, and when Luma's father caught sight of her, he asked, "Who are you?"

"I'm Charlie," she said. "I'm Luma's-" Friend? No, it was so much more than that. In a moment like this, there was no time to mince words so she just said, "I'm her girlfriend. Luma's been staying with me. Tabitha tried to kill her."

And she might have succeeded this time, Charlie thought, but immediately shoved the idea out of her head.

"What happened?" Luma's father asked. His eyes were wild and Charlie wondered how on earth she would be able to catch him up on everything that had happened in the last three weeks as they followed Luma out to the ambulance.

It seemed impossible.

"Tabitha happened," Charlie said. "She did this."

Shock rippled over Luma's father's face, and then something darker—like it didn't take a great amount of mental gymnastics for him to get to a world in which that was possible. He nearly fell down on the staircase and Charlie caught him, keeping him on his feet.

"Oh God," he said. "My baby girl."

"Come on," Charlie said, guiding him down the stairs. "I'll bring you to the hospital."

"Thank you," Luma's father said weakly.

She helped him outside, then when she explained her truck was all the way down the street, Luma's father nodded to the slick black Town Car parked in the drive. "My driver will take us. You've been taking care of my daughter?"

Charlie nodded wordlessly.

"Thank you," Luma's father said. As Charlie was getting into the back of the car, she saw sirens in the distance, coming to collect Antonio. They'd be going after Tabitha at the funeral home, too, based on what Charlie told the 911 operator.

23

LUMA

Luma woke up in a dark room.

She opened her mouth to scream, expecting Tabitha to come lunging out of the darkness at any moment, but her throat felt like it was on fire. The pain cut her words off before they even passed her lips and panic rose in her throat.

What was going on? Where was she?

Luma sat up and felt soft fabric beneath her, hard plastic railings on either side of her hips. She ran her hands along them until her fingertips tripped over something rubbery and flexible. She followed it and found a small, round hospital call button draped over her right thigh.

The hospital?

She pushed both of the small round buttons on the device. One of them turned on an overhead light above the bed and the other made a chime in the distance.

The room Luma was in was empty – there was an armoire pushed up against one wall, a TV across from her bed, and a window on another wall, but no light came from it. It was night, and the last thing Luma remembered was opening her father's study door.

That must have been around noon, and the harder she tried to fill in the blanks in the missing time, the more frustrated she felt. This was the second time she'd woken up with gaps in her memory in the last week and this time, Charlie wasn't even around to fill her in.

Oh God.

"Charl-" she started to say, wincing and putting her hand to her throat as the word came out garbled. Her fingertips touched a cloth bandage and then recoiled as the muscles in her neck screamed in pain. Luma had no clue how she'd gotten into that hospital bed, but one memory from the afternoon did come back to her as sharp as if she was reliving it. She'd turned around on the stairwell and Charlie wasn't there, and then Luma had gone on without her.

Why didn't I go back for her?

She dropped the call button and threw off the blankets that were covering her legs. She had no idea what happened to her but she knew exactly who to blame, and she wasn't about to keep sitting there when Charlie could be in danger.

She fumbled with the rails of the hospital bed. There must have been a button to release them but

Luma couldn't find it, and she was about to climb over them when the door swung open.

Luma froze.

It's probably a nurse, she tried to reassure herself as her heart insisted she make a run for it. *You pushed the call button. It's just a nurse.*

It sounded totally logical. And yet, so did the other word swimming through her head. *Run.*

Luma had one leg thrown over the rail when she heard the sweetest voice in the world. "Luma!"

She looked up just in time to see Charlie drop a bottle of soda on the floor, the carbonation exploding the cap and sending fizzy liquid shooting across the room. Behind her was Luma's father, and on his tail, the nurse that Luma had paged.

"Charlie!" This time it came out as a recognizable word, but it was barely more than a whisper. "Dad!"

"She's conscious," the nurse said. "That's incredible."

Me? Luma thought. This woman was looking at her as if she was witnessing a miracle and Luma wondered just how badly Tabitha had attacked her. The nurse went back to the doorway, hopping over the soda quickly this time, and called for a doctor, then Charlie and her dad both rushed to her bedside. Charlie had the railing down in a millisecond, wrapping Luma protectively in her arms and practically crawling into the bed with her. Luma felt her tears hot against her neck as she murmured, "I knew you weren't going to leave me like that."

"Never," Luma croaked. She looked over Charlie's shoulder to see her dad standing near the foot of her bed, looking like he was afraid she might break if he came too close. She held out her hand and whispered, "Dad."

"Baby," he said, taking her hand. "I was so worried, I thought you were dead."

"I'm sorry," Luma tried to say.

"Don't try to talk," her dad answered. "I'm the one who's sorry. I should have seen the viciousness in that woman. I should have known she was behind your disappearance."

The nurse returned with a doctor in tow and Charlie and Luma's father stepped aside so they could check on Luma's vitals. The doctor was a sleepy-looking woman in a white lab coat who introduced herself as Dr. Anderson. She and the nurse did a few tests and asked, "Do you know where you are?"

"Hospital," Luma rasped. She opened her mouth to speak again. She had so many questions, but they all hurt to ask.

"What year is it?" The doctor asked, and Luma looked at Charlie. *Really? It was that bad?*

Charlie stepped forward and took her hand, and Luma's dad said, "It's okay."

When Dr. Anderson was done checking Luma over,

she said, "Ms. White, you're a very lucky girl, and you almost certainly wouldn't be alive right now if it weren't for the fast thinking of this incredible young woman."

Luma looked at Charlie, falling as always into those incredible aquamarine eyes, and nodded. Luma might not know what happened, but she didn't doubt that Dr. Anderson was right about her. Charlie had been saving her ever since they met.

"What happened?" Luma managed to ask.

"You were found unresponsive in your home, with evidence of strangulation around your neck," Dr. Anderson said. "The paramedics intubated you and were able to get your heart started again with a defibrillator, but you were without oxygen for a long time. We weren't sure if you were going to regain consciousness, but it looks like you've miraculously made it out without sustaining any brain injury. We'll do some more tests in the morning to find out for sure, but it looks like you're okay."

"Thank you," Luma managed to say.

"The soreness will go away in a few days," the doctor reassured her. "In the meantime, you should keep hydrated. Sucking on ice chips might help."

"I've already got some," Charlie said eagerly, pointing to an ice bucket on a tray table at the foot of the bed. "Just got some fresh ice about an hour ago in case Luma woke up."

"You should get some rest now, Ms. White," Dr.

Anderson said. "It's late, and the police will have questions for you in the morning."

She patted Luma's shoulder reassuringly, then led the nurse out of the room. The nurse paused in the doorway and pointed to the soda on the floor, saying, "I'll call someone to clean this up."

"I'm sorry about that," Charlie said. "I got excited."

"It's okay, dear," the nurse said.

Then she was gone again and Luma croaked, "Tabitha?"

"In police custody," her father hurried to reassure her. "She's never going to be able to hurt you again." Luma nodded, then her dad said, "The nurse is right. It's about two in the morning and you should get some more rest. Do you need anything?"

Luma shook her head.

"I've bribed my way into an empty room down the hall," her father said. "I'm just two doors down if you need me, and I got Charlie a bed in the room next to yours." He put his hand on Charlie's shoulder and said, "The doctor was right—she's a great girl and I'm never going to be able to repay her for saving you."

"I love you, Dad," Luma said.

"I love you so much, honey," her father said, leaning over the bed to hug her. He left the room reluctantly and then she and Charlie were alone.

"Do you want me to go so you can rest?" Charlie asked.

"No," Luma said, twisting her hand into the fabric of Charlie's shirt to prevent her from leaving. "Stay."

Luma pulled Charlie by her shirt, bending her over the bed until their lips met. Luma never knew she could miss anyone as much as she did in the minutes that she'd been alone in her hospital bed and worrying about what happened to her. *Thank you, thank you, thank you,* Luma repeated to herself, a silent prayer to the universe for being on their side.

Charlie kissed her back with passion and urgency, her lips salty from dried tears. When she pulled back, she said, "I love you." Her words were punctuated by a thousand little kisses. "Luma, I was so worried I wasn't going to get the chance to tell you that, but it's true – I love you more than I ever thought possible."

"I-" Luma started to say, grimacing at a metallic taste in her throat.

"Shh," Charlie said, pulling back a little bit so she could look into her eyes. "Just nod. Do you love me, too?" Luma nodded emphatically and a huge grin broke over Charlie's face. "I knew it."

Luma pointed to the water cup on the tray table at the foot of the bed and Charlie filled it from a pitcher, then scooped some ice chips into it along with a straw. She held it for Luma as she drank. That part wasn't necessary – there was nothing wrong with her arms – but Charlie seemed happy doing it so Luma let her. When the cup was empty, Luma smiled and said, "I love you, too."

Charlie was beaming and Luma relaxed against the pillow, opening her arms for Charlie to join her.

"Think the nurse is going to have a problem with it?" Charlie asked, glancing toward the hallway.

Luma shook her head and then croaked, "I don't care."

Charlie snuck over to the door, closing it before coming back and kicking off her sneakers to climb into bed beside Luma. Charlie put her arm around her and Luma nestled into the curve of her body. Charlie kissed her forehead, then the tip of her nose, and snuggled Luma closer to her. Relieved, she hit the button to turn off the light above the bed and they settled into a surprisingly peaceful sleep together.

24

CHARLIE

It was early in the morning when Charlie felt Luma stirring beside her. She'd slept the whole night in the crook of Charlie's arm and even though her back was sore and everything from her shoulder down was numb, Charlie had no interest in moving a muscle.

Charlie opened her eyes as Luma squirmed against her, her body reacting with a surge of desire before she realized the reason for Luma's movement. There was a nurse at the bedside, whispering, "Good morning, dear. Sorry to wake you – I just need to check your vitals."

"It's okay," Luma said, holding out her arm for the woman to take her pulse. "Thank you."

So sweet, so pure... how could anyone do what Tabitha had done to her, and three times no less? Charlie let down the railing on her side of the bed and slid off, giving the nurse room to do her job. Charlie poked her head down the hall to tell Lucca that his daughter was awake, and when she came back, the nurse was checking the reactions of Luma's pupils. She took her temperature and asked her a few orienting questions as she worked. Charlie studied the nurse's face closely but she didn't see any signs of concern.

"How's she doing?" She asked when the nurse was done.

"Just fine," the nurse said. Then she turned to Luma and asked, "How's your throat feeling this morning?"

"Still scratchy," Luma said, her voice a little husky. "But better." She put her hand to the bandage and asked, "How long do I need to wear this?"

"You can take it off now if you're ready," the nurse said. "It's just there for a little bit of extra protection, but if you'd rather not-"

"I'd *love* to take it off," Luma said, reaching behind her head and trying to find the beginning of the bandage. She was talking easier this morning, but her voice was very hoarse and nothing like her usual lyrical tone. "I kept dreaming last night that her hands were on me-"

She stopped, a startled look in her eyes, but instead of letting her linger on that horrible memory, Charlie said, "Turn around. I can help you with that."

"Honey," Lucca said as he appeared in the door. "How are you feeling today?"

"Better," Luma said.

Lucca came over and hugged Luma, then shook Charlie's hand. He was surprisingly down-to-earth – Charlie noticed that yesterday when they were waiting together at the hospital. Charlie figured a man of his wealth and position would treat Charlie with the same dispassion as the hospital staff, or worse.

But the first thing he'd done after the doctor told them Luma was alive and stable was pull Charlie into a giant bear hug and thank her profusely. They kept each other company after that, waiting for Luma to wake up, and they'd been taking turns going on runs to the cafeteria. It had been Charlie's turn when Luma finally woke up.

Charlie gestured to the bandage and Luma turned to let her remove it. Charlie found the small butterfly clasps keeping the bandages around Luma's neck, popped them off and put them in the nurse's outstretched hand. Then Charlie unwound the bandage from Luma's neck. It was circled at least three times around and she seemed impatient to be free of it so Charlie worked as fast as she could.

As the last layer gave way to bare skin, Charlie tried not to gasp.

The dark purple bruise that bit into her delicate neck was all the more brutal-looking because of how fair her skin was, and Charlie could even see the outline of the necklace Tabitha had used. *That evil bitch.* Her whole body tensed with hatred and she lost herself in it for a moment, but then the nurse tapped Charlie's shoulder.

"Give the bandage here, dear," she said. "I'll dispose of that."

Charlie did as she was instructed and then the nurse asked Luma if she was ready for breakfast.

"Could I just get something to drink? Orange juice?" Luma asked.

"Oh, you don't want anything that acidic right now, trust me," the nurse said. "How about a nice smoothie instead? It'll soothe your throat and get some nutrients back into you before you waste away, dear."

"Thank you," Luma said, nodding.

The nurse dropped the bandages into a medical waste bin near the door and then disappeared, then Luma took Charlie's hand.

"Thanks for staying the night with me," she said.

"I couldn't leave you if I tried," Charlie told her.

"Dad," Luma croaked. "How did you sleep?"

"A lot better knowing you were just down the hall," Lucca said, patting Luma's other hand. While they waited for Luma's breakfast to arrive, he examined the ligature marks on Luma's porcelain skin and a few tears slid down his cheeks. "Your neck. I am so sorry. I should have protected you."

"It's not your fault, Dad," Luma said. "Neither of us knew she was capable of this."

Lucca gestured to the tray table at the end of the

bed and said, "Those things have mirrors in them sometimes. Do you want to see it?"

He inspected the tray table, pulling on the top. Just as he suspected, it lifted to reveal a vanity mirror. It caught the morning light from the window, sending a sunbeam briefly across Luma's face, and she winced as she caught a glimpse of her reflection.

"No," she said before Lucca could pull the table closer to her.

"What's wrong?" He asked.

"I don't want to be like her," she said. "I don't need to see it."

"You're not vain," Charlie said, squeezing Luma's hand. "You could never be like her."

"Please put the mirror away," Luma insisted, and her dad closed the tray table.

"Tabitha will pay for this," Lucca said, and then the nurse returned with Luma's smoothie. She handed a plastic cup to Luma along with a straw, then left the room and Lucca and Charlie both waited patiently while Luma downed about a quarter of her breakfast in one long, satisfied sip.

"What happens next?" she asked, her voice a little less froggy thanks to the icy smoothie.

"Are you feeling strong enough to give your statement to the police?" Lucca asked. "Charlie and I talked to them yesterday while you were sleeping, and that was enough to arrest Tabitha and Antonio. But they'll need your statement, too."

"I'll talk to them," Luma said, then she glanced down at her hospital gown and the bedding pulled up to her waist. "Not from this bed, though. Can you get me some real clothes and get me out of this bed? I want to go home."

"Of course," Lucca said, and Charlie held her breath, but neither of them missed a beat. "Charlie, you'll come with us, I assume?"

Charlie glanced at Luma, who was nodding enthusiastically. So she answered, "Yes. I'd like nothing more."

Lucca sent for some clothes from Luma's wardrobe at home, then started working on getting her discharged from the hospital. Charlie helped her into the bathroom and waited patiently while she showered, sitting on the bed and containing herself when all she really wanted to do was go into the bathroom, push aside the shower curtain and join Luma beneath the water.

She was even more sure that she loved Luma now that she'd almost lost her.

Charlie did find one constructive thing to do while she waited on Luma. She took her dad's phone out of her pocket and called her mother. She told her that everything was fine, and now that the danger passed, she was honest about their trip.

"Luma's stepmother attacked her again," she said. "She nearly died, and we're in the hospital right now."

"Oh my God!" Her mother exclaimed. "Are you okay?"

"Yes," Charlie said, her hand going to her back. It was still a little sore, but she'd heal soon. "We're both okay. Luma's getting discharged right now and we're going back to her house to give a statement to the police."

"Well, send her my love," Charlie's mom said. *My love, too,* she thought. Then her mom asked, "How long are you staying?"

"I'm not sure," Charlie said. "I'll keep you updated, though. Can you tell Scotty I'm not going to be at work on Monday?"

"Sure," her mom answered. "Stay safe, baby."

Charlie was just wrapping up her phone call when an older woman rapped her knuckles on the doorframe and walked into the room. "I've got Miss White's clothes."

"I'll take them," Charlie said. "Thank you."

The woman handed her a shopping bag, then left and Charlie went over to the bathroom door. She listened and the shower had been turned off, so she knocked. "Luma, your clothes are here."

She opened the door with a towel wrapped seductively around her waist, and Charlie smirked.

"What?" Luma asked.

Charlie shrugged. "My family would have sent

clothes in a used grocery bag, or an old backpack. Your family sends your clothes in Versace bags."

"Shut up and hand me the bag," Luma said with a wry grin.

Charlie did, and Luma disappeared again for a couple of minutes. She emerged wearing a pair of designer jeans and a ridiculously soft sweater that didn't do much to help Charlie keep her hands off her. She was looking a lot more like her old self – the rich girl with the nice clothes that Charlie had met on her first day in the forest before she'd put Luma in thrift store duds.

"You're so beautiful," Charlie said. Luma took her breath away.

"So are you," she said, coming over and pressing her body against Charlie. They kissed, then Luma tucked Charlie's bangs behind her ear and smiled. "Gorgeous."

"Come on," Charlie said before her hands had a chance to explore the curves of Luma's breasts in that soft sweater. "Your dad is waiting at the nurses' station."

When they joined him, he put his arm around Luma's shoulders and said, "I arranged to have a couple of officers meet us at the house in an hour so you can give your statement. Is that okay, honey?"

"Yes," Luma said. "I'm so ready to go home. Charlie?"

"I go where you go," Charlie said with a smile.

"You're all set," the nurse from earlier said, bringing a wheelchair around for Luma. When she saw the look in Luma's eyes, she said apologetically, "Hospital policy – you can get out of the chair as soon as you get to the curb."

Luma sat down reluctantly and the nurse stepped aside as Charlie took the handles of the wheelchair. Lucca led them down the hall to a row of elevators, which they took to the first floor. As the doors opened on the hospital lobby, he said, "I have to prepare you – there are reporters outside."

"Really?" Charlie asked.

"Yes," Lucca said. "Tabitha was arrested at the funeral yesterday and it was pretty eventful. There was already press there to cover the event, and that turned it into a bit of a media circus."

Luma seemed unfazed by this news – she just nodded and clutched the Versace bag containing yesterday's clothes a little closer to her chest. She was used to all this scrutiny and her world was in a completely different universe from Charlie's.

"You don't have to talk to them," Lucca said, mostly for Charlie's benefit. "And in fact, we shouldn't until Luma gives her statement to the police. Just keep your head down and head for the car – it's parked right outside."

"Okay," Charlie said, feeling a little jittery. It felt like going into a warzone. She pushed the wheelchair out of the elevator and they turned toward the hospital entrance. Charlie could see a crowd of about a dozen people on the sidewalk and a few of them took pictures, the flash of their cameras going off when they spotted Luma. Charlie stopped pushing her. "Whoa. Is that a news van?"

"I think so," Lucca said, sounding almost disinterested. "It's okay – they can be kind of pushy but they won't bite."

"I'm not worried about that," Charlie said. "Could we end up on the evening news?"

"Could, and probably will," Luma said. "Do you want to try to sneak out another door?"

"No," Charlie said. "I'm just glad I already called my mom. She'd kill me if she found out what happened from the news."

25

LUMA

Talking to the police was exhausting and Luma's throat was sore all over again by the time she was finished telling them everything she knew – from the day Antonio drove her into the woods to the moment she lost consciousness in her father's study with Tabitha's hands around her neck.

Charlie was right beside her the whole time, holding her hand, and when the police had gotten everything they needed from Luma, she got up to get her a glass of cold water from the kitchen. Luma was reluctant to let her hand go, and Charlie squeezed reassuringly.

"I'll be right back," she said. "Promise."

"Okay," Luma said.

Charlie left the room and then it was just Luma, her father, and the two officers that had taken her statement. They were finishing up their notes and getting ready to leave. Luma looked at her dad, giving him a sympathetic smile, then asked, "How are you feeling?"

Luma's throat was croaky again like it had been in the hospital and she was looking forward to Charlie's return – mostly because no matter how many police officers were in the house, she felt safer with her nearby, but also because she pretty badly needed that water.

"Oh, honey," her dad said, his expression softening for the first time since Luma started to give her statement. "After everything you've been through, you're worried about *me*?"

"Tabitha is your wife," Luma said. "This isn't only happening to me."

He moved his chair a little closer and took Luma's hand, patting it reassuringly. "I'm doing fine – as long as I know you're okay, that's all that matters to me. I'm so glad you had Charlie to help you through all of this and you didn't have to do it alone."

Charlie came back into the room and Luma's dad let go of her hand so she could take the water glass.

Luma took a long, grateful sip, and then her dad said, "If you two are okay in here, I need to make some calls to cancel the charity gala. There are over 200 RSVPs, and the caterers, and-"

"What if we don't cancel it?" Luma asked.

Her dad and Charlie both looked at her with confusion. Her dad said, "It was your stepmother's idea. She wanted to use your trust fund – Lord, when I think of what she must have *really* had planned for that money… it makes me sick."

"Dad," Luma said, trying to soothe him. "It's okay. What she did was horrible, but she didn't get away with it. It all turned out okay, and I was thinking that we could have the gala after all – turn this terrible ordeal into something positive." She took another sip of water to wet her throat, then went on. "We should turn the gala into a party. I'm alive and I feel like celebrating that fact. Plus, it's for a good cause."

The idea had begun incubating in Luma's mind on the ride home from the hospital. As soon as they pulled into the driveway, she saw a cloud form over Charlie's expression and Luma knew her well enough to know exactly what was bothering her – she didn't think she belonged in her world, and she was sort of right. The thing was, Luma didn't belong in it anymore, either. She wasn't sure she ever had.

"That's your trust fund," her dad objected. "The money belongs to you."

"I think this is the best way to spend it," Luma said, studying her dad for signs that he was offended. She hurried to add, "I really appreciate you setting that money aside for me, but you know I've always struggled to belong here."

"That was Tabitha making you feel unwelcome," her father said. "I should have seen it years ago."

"No," Luma insisted. "It was me. It took moving out to the forest, losing everything and finding Charlie to realize that. I don't want to rely on a trust fund my whole life—I want to make my own way."

"What about the modeling contract?" Her dad asked. Charlie seemed equally interested in this answer.

"I'm going to rip it up," Luma said. "I doubt they're still interested in me after waiting three weeks for an answer, anyway, and that was Tabitha's dream, not mine."

"If you're sure this is what you want," Luma's dad said. Luma nodded, and he said, "Okay. We'll go ahead with the gala."

"Can you add a few more attendees to the guest list?" Luma asked. She looked at Charlie and said, "Eight—your brothers and your parents?"

Charlie nodded and Luma's dad said he'd make it happen. Then he sighed and said, "Well, if you'll excuse me, I think I need a long shower and a nap. You two should do the same – Luma, you must be exhausted."

"I am," she agreed. They watched Luma's dad head out of the dining room and go up the stairs, then Luma turned to Charlie, wincing. "I'm sorry. I didn't mean to spring that charity stuff on you, or the gala. Do you think your family will want to come?"

"Are you kidding?" Charlie asked. "I'm sure they'll love it." She wrapped Luma in her arms and kissed her hard, then asked, "Were you serious about your trust fund? How could you turn away from all of this?"

She gestured around the grand dining room but Luma's eyes didn't follow hers. She kept her gaze on Charlie and when she looked at her again, Luma said, "I meant every word. All I want and all I need is you."

"So..." Charlie said, quirking her eyebrow up with an adorable look of confusion. "What does that mean for us? Rockledge is three hours away from Grimm Falls."

"I've helped out with a few charities that my dad is involved in and I know what it takes. A lot of the day-to-day stuff could be done online and over the phone. I don't need to be here, except to visit my dad," Luma said.

"What are you saying?" Charlie asked. "You want to move to the forest with me?"

"We could get an apartment in Grimm Falls to start with," Luma suggested. "You can work on growing your pottery business, I can run the charity." She trailed off, realizing just how crazy her plans were. She grinned and added, "I mean if you're not sick of all my drama by now."

"I *love* your drama," Charlie said. "And I love you."

"I love you, too," Luma said, throwing her arms around Charlie and momentarily forgetting how sore her neck was as she tilted her head to meet Charlie's lips. She winced and Charlie saw it.

"How are you feeling?"

"Never been better," Luma said. She gave Charlie

a look and said, "Although, I do like the idea of a bubble bath. Come upstairs with me?"

"You don't have to ask me twice," Charlie said. She took Luma's hand and let her lead the way upstairs to Luma's private bathroom.

It was nothing like Tabitha's dressing room, modest in relation but with a full-sized Jacuzzi tub in the corner. Charlie closed the door while Luma went over to it and started running the water for a bath. Charlie stopped her, taking her by the hand and leading her over to a dressing chair at a vanity table against one wall.

"You just rest," she said. "I'll run the bath for you."

Luma sat reluctantly, saying, "I'm perfectly capable of taking care of myself."

Charlie smiled at her. "I know. You proved that beyond a doubt. But let me take care of you now."

So Luma sat and Charlie tested the water, then added bubbles. When the bath was ready, she crossed the bathroom and held out her hand for Luma, pulling her to her feet. Charlie pulled her into a hug, wrapping her arms protectively around her as she kissed her.

"You're perfect," she said.

"I've got a big, purple bruise around my neck," Luma pointed out.

"You're still perfect," Charlie said. She kissed her softly, then slowly undressed her, kissing every inch of Luma's body as she let piece after piece of her clothing drop to the floor. Then, on her knees in front of her naked, beautiful girlfriend, she said, "You have no idea how hard it is not to take you right now."

Luma licked her lips – like she knew just how torturous the gesture would be for Charlie – and then Charlie got back to her feet.

"But you need to relax and get your strength back," she said, leading Luma over to the tub and helping her step into it. She bit her lip as she watched Luma's nakedness sink below the bubbly surface of the water, suds covering her breasts seductively.

"You could get in the bath with me if you wanted," Luma said, looking up at Charlie through her eyelashes. "You know, just to soak."

Charlie shook her head. "I really couldn't – I don't have that much self-restraint."

Luma smiled at her, then said, "Okay. Keep me company, then."

Charlie sat down on the edge of the tub, letting down the ponytail Luma had her hair in and massaging her scalp. Then she let her hands venture further down, skipping over her tender neck and settling on Luma's shoulders instead. She massaged her gently, slowly, enjoying the sensation as her hands dipped into the warm water and glided over Luma's slick, wet skin.

Luma let out a low moan that sent a tingle up Charlie's spine and reddened her ears. It was the sound of desire and Charlie felt herself getting wet with it, too.

She was good, though. Luma had just been

discharged from the hospital that morning and even though she was being strong, acting like none of it bothered her, Charlie knew she'd need time to heal. So she perched on the edge of the tub, carefully massaging Luma's shoulders and back and resisting the urge to slide her wet hands down over Luma's perfect breasts. She talked to Luma, telling her how proud she was of her and how grateful she was that Luma was okay.

And after a little while, she noticed that Luma was asleep. She'd gotten hardly any rest in the hospital – she was probably overdue for a good night's sleep. Charlie carefully extracted herself from behind Luma and got the vanity chair, bringing it to the side of the tub and watching Luma sleep peacefully.

The next time Charlie found herself standing in Luma's bathroom with her was a few days later. Luma was much more like herself, she'd been to see her doctor for a follow-up which she got through with flying colors, and the bruise on her neck was turning from purple to yellow as it healed.

And she was looking at Charlie with mischief in her eyes.

"What?" Charlie asked. "What are we doing in here?"

"There was something I wanted to do with you the

last time we were here," Luma said, then pouted playfully and said, "But you wouldn't let me."

"I wanted to make sure you were better first," Charlie said.

"I'm great now," Luma said. She went over to the bathtub and turned on the water, bending over at an exaggerated angle just because she knew Charlie couldn't look away from her. When she looked back, she got confirmation that Charlie was watching her – and practically drooling on the expensive tile floor.

Luma stood up and sauntered seductively across the floor, putting her arms around Charlie's neck. "I love you, Charlie."

"I love you, too, Luma," Charlie breathed, and Luma grabbed the tails of Charlie's shirt in her fists, lifting them then sliding her hands underneath to touch the warm, firm skin over her abdomen. Charlie turned to butter in her hands, a happy smile over her lips.

Luma took her time undressing Charlie, stripping her shirt first, and then her bra. She got to her knees as she pulled Charlie's jeans down and helped her step out of them, and then she looked up and locked eyes with Charlie as she took hold of her briefs and slid them slowly down her thighs.

She was already wet, ready for Luma.

Luma bit her lip, teasing Charlie, then brought her mouth to Charlie's clit. She wrapped her arms around Charlie's thighs, putting her hands on her firm ass as she felt Charlie's legs buckle and then regain their balance. Luma glided her tongue through Charlie's folds and settled on her clit again, and before long, Charlie had her head thrown back, letting out a series of low moans with each stroke of her tongue.

When Charlie's thighs began to quiver uncontrollably, Luma got to her feet. She took Charlie's hand to guide her over to the edge of the tub so she could continue, but Charlie had other ideas. She stripped Luma bare, making much shorter work of it than Luma had, then lay down a towel across the back of the bathtub so Luma wouldn't feel the cold tile on her skin.

Charlie sat her down on it, then she stepped into the bath, submerging herself before coming up again and wrapping her arms around Luma. She was wet and slick from the bubbles, and their bodies glided together in the most sensual and exciting way.

Luma gathered droplets of water from Charlie's skin with her tongue, lapping at her neck and her earlobe until Charlie's thighs were shaking again. Charlie's hand went between Luma's legs and she happily spread her thighs around Charlie's hips.

As Charlie penetrated her, Luma moved her body to meet Charlie's hand, sliding back and forth over the wet tile and using it as momentum to make Charlie's hand pump into her faster, harder. Charlie reacted hungrily, nibbling on Luma's earlobe, her jaw, her lower lip, and ignoring the water as they created waves that sloshed over the edge of the tub.

Luma came first, clinging to Charlie as she slid along the tile and rode her hand. Then she slipped over the edge of the tub and into the water, her hand seeking Charlie to pick up where she'd left off. By the time they were done, there were more suds on the floor than in the tub and Luma lay against Charlie's chest in the bathtub. Charlie ran her hands slowly, almost lazily over Luma's breasts, making her nipples stand at attention and dipping her head to kiss Luma's neck.

"You're going to make me want you again," Luma murmured, feeling another wave of desire build in her core.

"Please," Charlie said. "Never stop wanting me."

Luma twisted around to face Charlie and said, "Never."

Then her hand found Charlie's body again beneath the surface of the water.

EPILOGUE
CHARLIE

To say the gala was a grand event was a gross understatement to Charlie's small-town sensibilities.

Lucca had rented an enormous banquet hall with beautiful stone architecture from the turn of the century, there was a live band playing on stage, and expensive crystal everywhere Charlie looked. And she spotted more than a few celebrities throughout the night.

None of them could hold a candle to Luma, though.

Even with her tender, bruised neck, she was radiant and she seemed to suck all the air out of the cavernous room whenever Charlie looked at her. Luma wore a long, glittering dress of golden yellow, and whether she was in an expensive ball gown or an old t-shirt, she was still the most beautiful girl Charlie had ever seen.

Charlie was in a suit—the nicest one she'd ever worn thanks to Luma, who had taken her into downtown Rockledge the day before the gala to buy it. Charlie's brothers and father were there, too, and Luma insisted on outfitting all of them in whatever they wanted as her way of thanking them for their kindness. Then Luma and Charlie took Charlie's mom to buy a cocktail dress to match her husband's cornflower blue tie.

Charlie tried to object to all of it, but Luma wouldn't hear it.

"I spent a hundred dollars on the clothes I bought you in Grimm Falls," she reminded Luma as they stood at the cash register and Luma pulled out a credit card. "This is too much—lumberjacks don't wear formalwear in the forest. We can all rent suits for the gala."

"You could," Luma said, running her hand along Charlie's jawline. "But a nice suit will last a long time and you never know when you'll need it. Let me do this for you and your family. I want to."

So the Jacobs clan arrived at the gala in style. Joey and Braden brought their girlfriends from Grimm Falls, and Charlie was surprised to see how quickly they all assimilated themselves into the crowd. Charlie caught Adam flirting with a movie star at one point, and even Maxwell got on the dance floor after a drink or two.

And Charlie stuck by Luma the whole night, admiring the way she moved effortlessly between their two worlds. When it was time to make the official announcement to introduce the Luma White Search and Rescue Foundation to the world, Charlie tried to let go of her hand and let her go up to the stage herself, but Luma wouldn't let go.

"Come on," she said. "You're a part of this, too, and I want you up there with me." She gave Charlie a quick kiss, then teased, "Unless you have stage fright?"

"Not with you beside me," Charlie said, and they went to the podium together. Charlie held her hand the whole time Luma was explaining the history behind the charity. She spared no details, and Charlie caught sight of Lucca in the audience, beaming proudly at his daughter.

Luma gave an account of what had happened to her and ended her speech with, "The Luma White Search and Rescue Foundation will provide vital training to law enforcement and volunteer search and rescue parties alike because everyone who's lost deserves to be found."

Then she pulled Charlie into a kiss, right there on the stage.

I t was on their six-month anniversary that Charlie found herself being led through the forest, her hand in Luma's and autumn leaves crunching beneath her feet.

They'd been attached at the hip ever since the gala. They stayed in Rockledge during Tabitha's trial and conviction, and helped Lucca through the emotionally trying process of filing for divorce. Antonio pled no contest at his arraignment and was serving jail time, too, but the judge had been more sympathetic toward him than with Tabitha, and he'd be out in a couple of years.

Luma's story became a national news sensation and reporters followed all of them for weeks until the criminal trials were over. Charlie figured her parents would be mad when they found out the extent of her involvement, but instead, they saw her the same way the news was portraying her—as a hero who saved the love of her life.

Charlie and Luma came back to Grimm Falls after all of that was over. They got an adorable little apartment above a bakery in town and every morning, they woke to the smell of fresh donuts and the birds chirping outside their window. Charlie finished her mug order and Rhonda was over the moon with her creations. Luma had insisted that Charlie not deliver the silly little mug they'd made together, so it took pride of place on the kitchen windowsill where they could both see it every day and be reminded of when they first met.

The Magic Bean closed for a couple of weeks for renovations, and Charlie took Luma to the grand opening so they could be two of the first customers to drink out of Charlie's mugs. Luma ordered a toffee nut coffee and smiled blissfully while she drank it.

"Yep," she said, "definitely tastes better in a Charlie Jacobs mug."

Charlie's chest had swelled with pride, and then to her surprise, she'd been inundated with orders. People really loved the hand-crafted quality of The Magic Bean's new mugs, and someone in the group of reporters that had been following Luma's story picked up on it, too. Charlie got a feature in a national magazine, and the orders were coming in faster than she could fill them.

Meanwhile, Luma's charity work was going wonderfully, she'd raised even more money to supplement her trust fund, and she was already receiving recognition for it. Just a month ago, she'd made a connection with the teen center in Grimm Falls and was looking forward to collaborating with the coordinator there.

Life was good.

No, it was *great*.

"Where are we going?" Charlie asked for the tenth time since they'd parked Luma's car on the shoulder of the highway and started hiking.

"I already told you," Luma said, laughing. "It's a *surprise.*"

"Well, are we almost there?" Charlie asked.

"You're terrible at surprises, you know that?" Luma teased. She stepped behind Charlie's back and reached up to cover her eyes. "As a matter of fact, we are almost there. Just another minute or two."

"You want me to walk through the forest with my eyes closed?" Charlie asked. "I'm going to trip."

"I would never let that happen," Luma said. She smelled like warm vanilla and Charlie wanted to stop walking just so Luma would crash into her. But they kept going, and after about a minute of carefully making their way down the dirt path, Luma said, "Okay, stop."

Charlie did and brought her hands up to Luma's to try to pry her fingers apart.

Luma laughed and chastised, "No peeking. Do you know where we are?"

"The apple orchard?" Charlie guessed.

"Close," Luma said, then she uncovered Charlie's eyes.

They were standing in front of the little cabin Charlie had taken Luma to after she'd eaten the poisoned apple. Except it wasn't the same dilapidated, ugly house with rotting wood that it was six months ago. It had been completely restored, with freshly painted wood siding, brand new windows, and even a couple beds of flowers on either side of the mint-colored front door.

"Luma," Charlie breathed. "What did you do?"

"The only thing I could think of to show you just how much I love you," Luma said. Then she shrugged and added, "I had a lot of help. Remember how I kept going into Rockledge every Monday to run search and rescue training sessions?"

"Yeah," Charlie said. "You would never let me come because you said they were boring and I had orders to fill."

"Well, I fibbed," Luma said. "I've been coming out here to work. Your brothers all sacrificed one day a week to help me fix this place up. They donated the wood and I learned how to hang siding."

"Really?" Charlie asked, a huge grin on her face.

"Don't look so surprised," Luma said, nudging Charlie with her elbow. "I'm handy."

"Clearly," Charlie said, looking back at the cabin. "It's beautiful."

"I'm glad you think so," Luma said. "Do you want to look inside?"

"Of course," Charlie said. "So does this mean you want to live out here with me? Did I pull a Grandpa Jacobs without even trying?"

Luma laughed and said, "Not quite. Come on, I'll show you."

She led Charlie to the door, where there was another surprise waiting for her. Charlie stopped in her tracks, feeling a little breathless. There was a wood plaque hanging just above the door with the words *Charlie Jacobs Pottery* carved into it.

"Did my dad make that?" She asked.

Luma nodded, then pushed the door open and said, "Charlie, this is your new studio. There's a workbench and your pottery wheel in the living area, and Scotty and Adam moved your kiln from the cottage to the back yard."

Charlie stepped into the cabin, taking everything in. Not only had they fixed up the outside, but Luma and her brothers had completely renovated the interior as well. The kitchen had new appliances and a nice butcher block countertop, there were a dining table and couch for relaxing, and the original wood floors had been refinished. Her pottery wheel had the place of honor, right in the middle of the living area with a nice view out the window to the forest.

"What do you think?" Luma asked.

"It's perfect," Charlie said. "Where did you get the money for all this?"

Luma smiled sheepishly and said, "The Bank of Dad. I was going to do it all myself—I would have gotten the money, but it definitely wouldn't have happened in six months. When you got that magazine feature and your business started to pick up, my dad offered to pay for it as his thanks for everything you did for me. Well, *offered* isn't really the right word. When Lucca White decides something, it happens."

"I'll have to thank him profusely the next time we go to Rockledge," Charlie said. She wrapped her arms around Luma's waist, picking her up and twirling her around as she added, "And I'll have to thank you profusely right now."

When she put Luma back down on her feet, she winked at Charlie and said, "Well, if that's what you want, there's one more room you haven't seen yet."

She nodded to the bedroom where Charlie had nursed her back to health. The door was closed and Luma took Charlie's hand, pulling her over to it.

She put her hand on the knob and said with a seductive grin, "I figured we might need a special place for when I come to watch you work. I don't think I can watch you shape clay in your hands without getting a little turned on."

Luma pushed the door open to reveal a quaint little bedroom, not very large but big enough to hold a queen-sized bed at its center.

"A *little* turned on?" Charlie teased, putting her hands around Luma's waist and pushing her through the doorway.

"Just a little," Luma said, wrinkling her nose.

Charlie sat her down on the edge of the bed, kicking the door shut as she crawled on top of Luma. "I love you so much. Thank you for this."

"I love you, too, Charlie," Luma said, and she was already pulling Charlie's shirt over her head. They made love with the window open, a cool fall breeze blowing the curtains and a cardinal singing on a branch nearby.

THE END

More from Cara Malone

If you enjoyed the clash of Luma and Charlie's very different worlds coming together in *Fairest,* I think you'll love *When Stars Align,* which features a rock star and an athlete getting a second chance at love.

Read it now in Kindle Unlimited

SNEAK PEEK: CINDERS

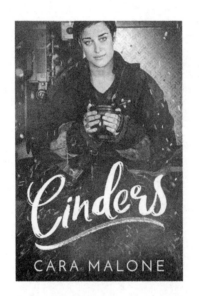

C ynthia Robinson arrived at the museum in style – hanging off the side of a fire truck with sirens blaring. It was how she would choose to travel anywhere, if she had her way, because the sound of the sirens and the weight of her uniform always got her adrenaline pumping.

As it turned out, it was a tad much for the situation at hand.

There was a class of third graders lined up in the parking lot, most of them with their noses in their phones and paying no attention at all to the screaming red fire engine as it pulled up to the curb. There were also a handful of volunteer docents, a security guard – who happened to be Cyn's stepbrother – and the museum director, a tightly wound man named Orson.

There was no smoke or flames to be seen, and the museum itself was quiet. Normally when the fire department got called, it was because the alarms inside the building in question had gone off, and they were usually still blaring when Cyn and her crew arrived. The only thing that was blaring today was Orson.

"I just don't understand how anyone could do such an awful thing!" he exclaimed as Cyn hopped off the truck and went to meet him. "It's simply unpatriotic!"

"Why don't you show us what happened?" Cyn asked, trying to sound calm and reassuring to balance out his frenetic energy. "Has the fire been contained?"

"Yes, I put it out myself," Orson said, puffing out his chest with pride. "I'm good in a crisis."

Who told you that lie? Cyn wondered. The way his whole body was practically twitching with distress gave her second-hand anxiety. She nodded to her step-brother, who was standing with the docents, looking bored and scratching the scraggly hair on his chin. "Come with us, Drew. You might be able to help."

He gave her a look that made it clear he was unenthusiastically obeying her order. They were never the loving type of step-siblings, and she knew taking orders from her got under his skin. That's why she was determined to be gentle and deferential when she asked him what he knew about the fire.

Cyn, Orson and Drew went inside the building, along with a couple of guys from her crew. The others stayed outside with the truck, winning over the kids by letting them play on it while they waited to find out if they would be needed.

It was strange to be alone inside the museum. It wasn't too long ago when Cyn herself was one of those third graders here on a field trip, and now it was her job to keep it safe.

Orson led the group down a few winding hallways until they got to the Local Artists exhibit, then he hung his head as he presented the charred remains of a canvas at the end of the hall. It was unrecognizable – a blackened and drippy mess of browns and grays where all the paint had either burned or melted into a homogenous goop.

Orson was right about one thing – an attack on the artwork of a Grimm Falls native felt like a personal attack on Cyn's own soul. Part of the reason she became a firefighter was to protect this town she'd come to love like it was a part of her.

"I blame myself," Orson said while Cyn pointed her guys to the canvas, instructing them to make sure the danger was past. "Although I don't know how I could possibly have predicted this. Who would be motivated to do something like this? I nearly vomited when I heard one of my docents yelling 'fire'."

"Did you see anything, Drew?" Cyn asked.

"No," he said. "I was keeping an eye on that group of elementary kids, making sure they kept their fingers off the art, you know?"

Cyn nodded, committing his response to memory, as well as everything else she saw and heard. Paintings didn't just spontaneously combust, so she'd have to write up a report for the fire investigator after they were done here. She'd been a firefighter for four years now, and she learned pretty early on that the smallest details sometimes make the biggest difference.

Like the way Orson was practically choking back sobs while he watched Cyn's crew inspect the canvas. Overacting? Maybe, but she'd seen a wide variety of stress reactions in the last few years and an abnormally large reaction to a relatively small event wasn't out of the ordinary. Especially considering how much the museum meant to Orson.

"Hey, Anthony Rosen," one of Cyn's guys – Gleeson – said as he read the name off a small, slightly blackened plaque on the wall. He turned and shot a mischievous grin at her as he asked, "Wasn't that your old high school flame?"

Cyn felt her cheeks coloring. She'd gotten used to the way the guys at the firehouse ribbed each other – and her – nearly constantly, but her history with Anthony wasn't a subject she liked to dredge up.

She was just trying to pick out the perfect snarky response when she heard someone behind her say, "Nice choice of words, asshole."

She turned to see her best friend, Gus, sauntering up the hall in his policeman's blues. *Thank you,* she thought, telepathically sending the message to him. Not that she needed rescuing, but there was nothing like a little police-firefighter rivalry to deflect attention from herself.

"I was just teasing old Cinders about her straight phase," Gleeson said, holding up his hands defensively. Then he grinned and said, "Anyway, I was thinking about motive. How did that relationship end, again?"

Cyn rolled her eyes heavily and said, "I caught him under the bleachers with another girl on prom night."

He quirked an eyebrow at her and said, "Sounds like revenge to me."

"A dish best served five years later?" Cyn asked.

Anthony certainly hadn't been in the running for any *World's Best Boyfriend* awards back then – that was for sure – but Cyn hadn't exactly given him a chance. Ever since she moved here, she'd only had eyes for the blue-eyed, blonde-haired, hopelessly out-of-reach Marigold Grimm. Anthony was nothing more than an attempt to appease her stepmother, and Cyn had been hurt when she found him kissing someone else under the bleachers, but the hurt didn't last long.

Certainly not five years after high school ended.

"He's a jerk," Drew said. "Probably had it coming from any number of people he's pissed off."

"Dude, I saw him get into a bar fight last weekend," Gleeson said. "Forgot about it until just now. I wasn't close enough to hear what it was about, but anybody mad enough to take a swing at a guy at the bottom of the ninth with two strikes is worth talking to."

"Good," Gus said, pulling out his notepad and flipping to a fresh page. "Do you know who it was?"

"Braden Fox. He's kind of a hot head, too. Definitely not the first bar fight he's ever been in."

That was one of the best things about Grimm Falls, in Cyn's eyes. It was a deceptively big city that felt a lot like a small town. Most everyone who stuck around long enough knew each other, and that was great if you wanted to feel safe leaving your door unlocked, or feel like a part of a genuine community.

Not so great if you wanted to go around getting in bar fights and setting paintings on fire without getting noticed.

"Thanks, I'll check him out," Gus said. Then he nodded at the charred canvas and said, "And we have to get the fire investigator in here. That was no accident."

Read Cinders now on Amazon

Printed in Great Britain
by Amazon

41782971R00175